COOKING CLIPS

STORIES OF
AND RECIPES FROM
THE PATRONS OF
THE JOHN MARSHALL BARBER SHOP

COMPILED BY

LINDA HENLEY
&
EBONY TALLEY

EDITED BY
BETH ANN COSBY CONNER
GORDON CONNER
BENNETT BROWN
BETHANY BROWN

THE OAKLEA PRESS

RICHMOND, VIRGINIA

Cooking Clips: Stories of and Recipes from the Patrons of The John Marshall Barber Shop © 2011 by Hugh M. Campbell. All rights reserved. Printed in the United States of America. No part of this book may be used or reproduced in any manner whatsoever without written permission except in the case of brief quotations embodied in critical articles and reviews. For information address The Oaklea Press Inc., 41 Old Mill Road, Richmond, Virginia 23226.

ISBN 10: 1-892538-56-3
ISBN 13: 978-1-892538-56-7

This book is dedicated to Mr. Hugh M. Campbell,
our "Knucklehead,"
who, for more than 40 years,
has served his clients with unwavering
loyalty and dedication.

With great admiration,
Your past and present employees,

Ebony Talley and Linda Henley

October, 2011

A Message from Hugh M. Campbell, the Current Owner

I was born in Staunton, Virginia, March 12, 1946, to the late Preston T. and Novella B. Campbell. I started my career as a barber in Downtown Richmond, Virginia, at the John Marshall Barber Shop. As the story has been told for many years now, I came to the John Marshall Barber Shop seeking only temporary employment. At the time, I needed a deferment to get into the air guard with my buddies. But because of the terrific relationships I build with my clients, many of whom are now my friends and golf buddies, what started out as temporary employment turned into a career lasting more than 40 years.

I'd like to acknowledge my gratitude to my lovely wife, Sharon, for supporting me in my career as a barber, as well as my two children, Brandon Campbell and Heather Davis; my three grandchildren, Chris Campbell, Collin and Megan; and my extended family, my staff, and last but not least, "My Golf Buddies."

Many thanks to each one of you for your love and support, and may God continue to bless every one of you.

Hugh M. Campbell
October, 2011

CONTENTS

INTRODUCTION 7

THE MOST IMPORTANT RECIPE 9

DRINKS 11

Bourbon Slush
Bartender General's Bloody Mary
Les "Famous" Whiskey Sours
Apple Pie Drink

GREAT BEGINNINGS & SNACKS 17

Peanut Butter Playdough
Les Mosher's Boursin Cheese
Southern Style Pimiento Cheese
Spinach & Sausage Appetizer
Broccoli Salad
Honeymoon Salad
Frost Lime Walnut Salad
Quick Frozen Salad
French Onion Soup
Southwestern Back Bean Salad
Crockpot Tortilla Soup
Hot Crab Meat Dip
Sausage Appetizer
Christmas Salad (Red and Green)
Pickle Bites
Spicy Cheese Straws
Broccoli Salad
Thayer Win's Lime Shrimp Salad
Bird Leg

ENTREES 39

Chicken Enchiladas
Bar-B-Que Chicken
Chunky Turkey Chili
Stuffing for Wild Duck
Remington Mallards
Smokehouse Spaghetti
Favorite chili
Slow Cooker Cranberry Pork Loin
Potato Sausage Foil Packs
Shrimp and sausage Creole
My Meatloaf
Lover's Loaf
Ron's World Famous Meat Loaf
Chicken with Dried Beef
Billy's Chili

Egg & Herring Roll Casserole
Ragu
Pasta Puttanesca (Sauce of the Streetwalker)
Chicken Casserole
Crispy Chicken with Orange Peel
Hot Ham Biscuits
Venison Roast
Sweet-N-Sour Kraut
Maryland Lump Crab Cakes
Crab Cakes
Argentine Shepherds Pie
Chicken Parmigiana
Chicken Divan
Crab Meat Casserole
Potato Cheese Casserole
Gramma Kruse's Italian Spaghetti
Western Baked Beans
Husband's Delight (Ground Beef & Noodle Casserole)
Chicken with Tomatoes and Feta
Barbecue (North Carolina Style)
Wonderful White Chili
Asparagus & Chicken Casserole
Grilled or Baked Salmon with Honey Mustard
Pesto Roast Beef Panini
Chesapeake Crab Casserole
Cyber Chili
Orange Chicken
Pakistani Seekh Kapab
Creole Beef Stew
Shrimp Boil
George Allen's Favorite Lasagna
Alma's White Bean Chicken Chili
Cottage Pie

SIDES 93

Squash Pudding
Hot Polish Potato Salad
Spinach Stuffed Squash
Corn Pudding
Baked Brie in Filo Cups

BREAD 101

Epstein Family Pumpkin Bread
English Muffin Casserole Bread
Bev Beadles' Crescent & Cinnamon Rolls
Corn Bread
Yellow Squash Muffins

Soup   **109**

Curried Lentil Soup
Santa Fe Soup
Kip's Oyster Stew
Lucky's Rockfish Chowder
Mexican Soup
Mexican Chicken Soup
Taco Soup

Sauces & Toppings   **119**

Ernesta's Red Sauce
Grilled Eggplant Marinara
Italian Beef Ragu
Cucumber Corinader Sauce
Cranberry Butter
Lip Smackin' Feta Vinaigrette
Honey Mustard Dill Sauce

Desserts   **129**

Blackberry Roll
My Mother's Pound Cake
Ice Cream Cake
Huxoll Apple Cake
Blueberry Boy Bait
Great Chocolate Cake
Pecan Shortbread
Ranger Cookies
Sour Cream Pound Cake
Corn Pudding
Baked Brie Filo cups
Apple & Cheddar Cheese Flan
Seven Layer Bars
Hay Stack Cookies
Chris Miller's Chocolate Pie
Coconut Pie
Grandmothers Pork Cake
Mac & Charlie Suskind's Magnificent Hot Fudge Sauce
Greg Suskin's Chewy Chocolate Chip Cookies
Best Gooey Brownies
Strawberry Topped Cheese Cake
Cottage Pie
Chocolate Cake
Apple Cake
Sweet Potato Custard Pie
Old Fashioned Boiled Custard
Alan's Gingersnaps
Chocolate Chip Cheesecake
Pecan Pie
Chocolate Guinness Cake
Cream Pie
Cream Cheese Frosting
Old Fashion Pound Cake
Rusinga's Banoffee Pie
Pumpkin Pie Cake
Chocolate Mousse Cake
Cucumber Coriander Yogurt Sauce
Ma's Good Ole Molasses Cookies
Brownie Torte
Rich Chocolate Cake
Susan Allen's Famous Cranberry Cookies

Opening Day

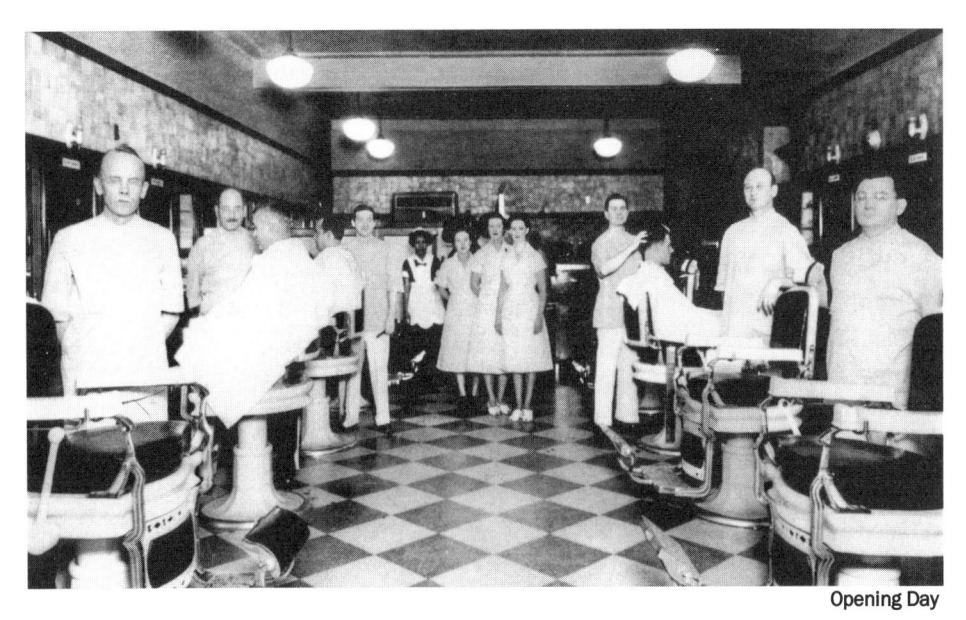

The John Marshall Barber Shop was established on October 29, 1929, in downtown Richmond inside the now historic John Marshall Hotel.

Over the years, there have been several owners. Mr. Hugh M. Campbell (the owner as of this writing) is still standing ... cutting and perpetuating the grand legacy of the true "barber shop" experience. Mr. Campbell, throughout his illustrious career, has served many distinguished patrons from all over the Commonwealth, as well as the United States. His goal of keeping and passing down the tradition of a "businessman's hair cut, a true hot cream shave, and a pleasant conversation" is still intact, because of his love of people, his even-keel demeanor, his down-to-earth sense of humor, and his superior customer service.

The John Marshall Barber Shop has evolved, since the Great Depression, for reasons other than great customer service. Because of its location in and affiliation with The John Marshall Hotel, at the corner of 5th and Franklin Streets, The John Marshall Barber Shop was forced to move into new quarters across the street from its original site.

Because the Hotel closed in 1988, re-opened in 1999, and then closed again in 2004, the Barber Shop took on new and different surroundings in the 21st Century.

These challenges, instead of weakening his conditions, have strengthened Mr. Campbell's resolve and business acumen, and his dedicated clients (and friends) continued to grow in number throughout these adjustments. The John Marshall Barber Shop was the last establishment to leave the dilapidated hotel building, and Mr. Campbell, along with his employees and their customers, eagerly await the historical landmark's major renovations, scheduled for completion in October, 2011.

On April 22, 2010, the construction crews' safety barriers surrounded the "old" Hotel, and its days and nights as visiting travelers' accommodations were forever gone.

Mr. Campbell, his employees, and their clients eagerly watched the historical landmark's transformation. With exciting changes having been made, its new tenants will dwell in luxurious Downtown apartments. They will seek the thrill of nearby blocks and blocks of good food, spirits, and entertainment and will appreciate the convenience of short jaunts to their places of work, among the many high-rises and cobblestone-laden streets.

HUGH M. CAMPBELL

The first retailer that committed to re-opening in the updated building was The John Marshall Barber Shop, and everyone (who's anyone) is anxiously awaiting its move back into its "old" digs ... but this time, within a "newly decorated, high-tech environment," complemented by its traditional flair for great clips of hair!

The inspiration to publish *Cooking Clips* comes from the various, daily personal conversations held within the walls of our establishment. It has been said, "The way to a man's heart is through his stomach." If this be at all true, then our hope is that this book of delicious recipes, shared over the sounds of buzzing, electric clippers and the buzz of excitement of anticipated dinner plans, will inspire you to try something new for your next meal!

Entertaining stories have touched our lives over many decades, and we trust that *Cooking Clips* will enrich your life, as you share meals with loved ones or cook simply for the joy of cooking (or because you're just good and hungry)!

This Book's Most Important Recipe:

The John Marshall Barber Shop Business Man's Hair Cut

1 Top Chef (The Barber)
1 Pair Andis® or Wahl® Clippers
1 Ounce of a Steady Hand
2 Cups All Natural Conversation
30 Minutes Away from the Office
1 Pinch of Jokes
4 Spoonfuls of the Past

Serves: Any Business Man

Combine all the above ingredients; marinate for 15 – 20 minutes. When done, you will receive 1 professional haircut.

For Dessert: The Tab

– by Linda Henley

DRINKS

Cooking Clips

BOURBON SLUSH

5 cups water
6 teabags
1+ cups sugar
12 oz. frozen orange juice concentrate (thawed)
12 oz. frozen lemonade concentrate (thawed)
2 cups Bourbon

Bring water to boil in large pot. Remove from heat; add tea; steep bags for 10 minutes and then discard them. Add sugar, orange juice, lemonade, and bourbon; stir well. Cover tightly and freeze at least 24 hours. Stir occasionally.

To serve: scoop into glass and add Sprite (or ginger ale) until consistency is "slushy."

"ENJOY! Good drink for Christmas instead of Eggnog."

Submitted by - Allan Lassiter

Cooking Clips

BARTENDER GENERAL'S BLOODY MARY

"This recipe was given to me by DuRoc Jones Batte, who, for many years, served as the Bartender General of the Sons of the American Revolution. He was charged with the early morning welfare of the Sons at their gatherings and, carefully, produced the drink one at a time."

1½ oz. vodka
4 oz. Mott's Clamato Juice
1 tsp. fresh lime juice
Dash celery salt
Dash freshly ground pepper
Dash Tabasco Sauce
Dash Worcestershire sauce
Garnish with lime wedge

May be served "on the rocks or straight-up."

Submitted by - Andy Nea

Cooking Clips

LES' "FAMOUS" WHISKEY SOURS

1 can frozen lemonade concentrate (yellow)
2 cans mixed orange juice (not concentrate)
1 can Bourbon or Rye Whiskey

Mix all in container and refrigerate. Serve over ice.

Submitted by - Les Mosher and Terry Louderback

Cooking Clips

APPLE PIE DRINK

1 gal. pasteurized apple cider
½ gal. apple juice
4 cups sugar
1 cup brown sugar
750 ml. "Everclear" grain alcohol (or corn liquor substitute)
8 Cinnamon sticks

Bring cider and juice to a boil. Add sugar and stir until dissolved. Reduce heat to simmer and add cinnamon sticks. Simmer 30-45 minutes. Cool to room temperature and add liquor. Bottle (old liquor bottles, wine bottles, cider and juice jugs, etc.) Can be served cold, room temperature or warm. "Sneaky good and warms your toes."

"Recipe was brought back from the Dakota states by a friend; it's starting to catch on in Virginia."

Submitted by - Lynn Chaffin, Martha, Caitlin, and Forrrest

GREAT BEGINNINGS & SNACKS

Cooking Clips

PEANUT BUTTER PLAYDOUGH

Ingredients:

1 cup peanut butter, any kind, crunchy or smooth
2/3 cup instant dry milk powder
¼ cup honey

In medium bowl, mix all ingredients together with hands or big spoon until smooth. Break off pieces and use cookie cutters to shape or roll in hands to make small balls. You can roll chips or chopped nuts, coconut, seeds, etc. or leave plain. Store in airtight containers in fridge. These are good eaten with sliced apples & yogurt for breakfast, lunch or snack.

Note: To the basic recipe, you can add wheat germ, oatmeal, raisins, mini-chocolate chips, or anything that tastes good with peanut butter.

Submitted by-Cabell Meadows – Age 7

LES MOSHER'S BOURSIN CHEESE

2 tbsp. margarine, softened
3 cloves garlic, minced and mashed (blend in with margarine)
12 oz. Philadelphia whipped cream cheese
1 tbsp. chives
2 tsp. dill weed
1 tsp. dry parsley

Mix all ingredients together with fingers and place in a serving bowl and refrigerate. Serve with an assortment of crackers.

Submitted by - Les Mosher and Terry Louderback

Cooking Clips

SOUTHERN STYLE PIMIENTO CHEESE

3 cups sharp shredded cheddar cheese (yellow & white mixed)
1 ½ cups chopped roasted red peppers (drained)
1 cup chopped olives
½ cup shredded Parmesan cheese
½ cup mayonnaise
3 tbsp. chopped parsley
½ tsp. black pepper
Cayenne pepper (to taste)

Combine all of the ingredients in a glass or stainless steel mixing bowl and mix well. Season to taste with cayenne pepper.

Refrigerate until ready to serve. Makes approximately 2 ¾ cups

Submitted by-Carl E. Vandergrift

Cooking Clips

SPINACH & SAUSAGE APPETIZER

2 packages of crescent rolls (8 per package)
12 oz. sausage (brown and drain)
(This is what the original recipe called for, but I just used the whole pound)
1 (10oz.) box of chopped spinach (microwave & drain)

Mix 8 oz. package of cream cheese with sausage and spinach, then add the following:
1 cup parmesan cheese
1 egg, beaten
Dash of Worcestershire sauce

Mix all ingredients well.

In an 8 ½" x 11" Pyrex dish (I used a 9" x 13"), layer 1 package. of crescent rolls on bottom; next spread all of the spinach/sausage mixture; then top with the other package. of crescent rolls. Bake at 350° F for 20-25 minutes.
Cut into squares and serve.

Submitted by-Jerry Lindquist

Cooking Clips

BROCCOLI SALAD

1 large head broccoli-cut in bite sizes
1 ½ cups shredded cheddar cheese
½ lb. bacon, cooked and crumbled
1 small onion, sliced through and left in rings
Mix together:
1 cup mayonnaise
½ cup sugar
4 tbsp. white vinegar

Pour over broccoli mixture and stir.

Submitted by-Tom & Linda Koertge

Cooking Clips

HONEYMOON SALAD

1 small package lemon gelatin (Jell-O brand)
1 small can Evaporated milk
1 (3 oz.) package cream cheese, room temperature
1 cup boiling water
1 small or medium can crushed pineapple*
*(if medium can, drain or drink some of the juice)
¼ cup sugar
2 tbsp. lemon juice
½ to 1 cup walnuts or pecans

Melt gelatin in cup of boiling water.
Beat with mixer - cream cheese and sugar.
Add lemon juice, and gradually, add evaporated milk – until smooth with no lumps.)
Add remaining ingredients and chill until set (overnight is best).

Submitted by-Carolyn and Randy Ridgely

Cooking Clips

FROST LIME WALNUT SALAD

1 small package (3 oz.) lime-flavored Jell-O
1 cup boiling water
1 (20 oz.) can crushed pineapple (undrained)
1 cup cottage cheese
¾ oz. cream cheese
½ cup diced celery
1 tablespoon chopped Maraschino cherries or strawberries
½ cup chopped English walnuts
1 tbsp salad dressing or mayonnaise

Add Jell-O gelatin to boiling water and stir until dissolved.

Cool until syrupy. Then add other ingredients and mix well. Pour into 8" square dish and refrigerate until solid.

When Jell-O gelatin is solid, frost with this mixture: ¾ oz. softened cream cheese. 1 tablespoon salad dressing or mayonnaise. Cream together and spread over top of gelatin salad.

Refrigerate until set, then decorate top, as desired with Maraschino cherries or strawberry slices and mint leaves.

Submitted by- Roscoe Puckett

Cooking Clips

QUICK FROZEN SALAD

1 package instant vanilla pudding
1 can fruit cocktail-drained
1 cup miniature marshmallows
½ to 1 cup pecans, chopped
1 small container Cool Whip

Make vanilla pudding as directed on package. Add well-drained fruit cocktail, fold in marshmallows and nuts. Lastly fold in slightly thawed Cool Whip until well mixed. May be frozen in a mold or loaf pan. Salad dressing may be added when served.

This recipe was submitted to a contest and won a cash prize and appeared in Better Homes & Garden magazine.

Submitted by- Jim & Mary Margaret Smith

Cooking Clips

FRENCH ONION SOUP

6 large white onions, julienned
½ container beef base
½ container French Onion Soup mix
1 cup (12 oz.) Sherry

Julienne onions and sauté in deep stockpot with butter until soft and translucent. Add water to cover (approx. 2 gallons), beef base and soup mix.
Simmer for half hour. Remove from heat and mix in sherry. Cool completely, store and label.

Submitted by-Terry Rose Oneill
Penny Lane Pub

Cooking Clips

SOUTHWESTERN BLACK BEAN SALAD

1 (15.5 oz.) can black beans, rinsed and drained
9 oz. frozen corn, thawed
1 tomato, chopped
1 small hass avocado, diced
¼ cup red onion, chopped
1 lime, juice of
1 tbsp. extra virgin olive oil
1 tbsp. cilantro
Salt and fresh pepper

Combine beans, corn, tomato, red onion, cilantro, salt and pepper.
Combine limejuice and olive oil. Mix with bean mixture.
Refrigerate for at least 30 minutes.
Add avocado before serving
Serves 12 (1/2 cup serving)

Cooking Clips

CROCKPOT TORTILLA SOUP

(This is from Southern Living Magazine and is so good you'll want to double this recipe; leftovers (if there are any) can be frozen.)

8 oz. chicken breast cubed, uncooked
2 cups frozen corn
1 large onion, chopped
2 cloves garlic, minced
4 cups chicken broth
10 ¾ oz. tomato puree (you can puree a can of diced or whole tomatoes in a blender)
10 oz. Rotel diced tomatoes/green chilies
1 tsp. salt1
1 tsp. cumin (ground Mexican spice)
1 tsp. chili powder
1/8 tsp. Cayenne pepper
1/8 tsp. black pepper
1 bay leaf
½ tsp. oregano

Toss all in crockpot on high; cook 6 hours.
Serve with shredded cheese and crushed tortilla chips

Submitted by-Becky and Wayne Hogue

Cooking Clips

HOT CRAB MEAT DIP

1 lb. fresh crabmeat, shells removed
1 (8 oz.) pkg. cream cheese, softened
½ pint sour cream
1 tbsp. lemon juice
1 tbsp. Worcestershire sauce
1 tsp. dry mustard
1 tsp. horseradish

Cream all ingredients except crabmeat. Fold in crabmeat. Pour in buttered or oil-sprayed/greased ovenproof dish. Bake at 325° for 30 minutes.

Submitted by - C. Wayne Anderson

Cooking Clips

SAUSAGE APPETIZER

Make extra of this, as it will go fast. Don't let appearance influence you...commonly called "throw up dip" but they'll keep coming back for more.

1 lb. Jimmy Dean Hot Sausage, cooked and crumbled*
1 can original Rotel Tomatoes and Green Chilies*
1 (7.5 oz.) jar red roasted peppers – chopped
1 (4 oz.) jar chopped pimentos
8 oz. cream cheese

*May use mild if too hot. Mix cooked sausage and cheese. Add other items and heat. Serve with dip chips such as "scoops".

Submitted by - Bruce Keeney

Cooking Clips

CHRISTMAS SALAD (RED AND GREEN)

¼ cup olive oil
2-4 tbsp. cider vinegar
1 tsp. soy sauce
Salt and pepper
Cooked beets
Spinach leaves
Shitake mushrooms
1 clove garlic
1 onion
Walnuts

Combine vinegar, oil, sugar, soy sauce and mix. Thinly slice beets, onions, and mushrooms. Sauté mushrooms with garlic in a little extra oil. Marinate beets, onions, garlic, and mushrooms in dressing. Serve over spinach and garnish with walnuts.

Submitted by - Steve and Dianne Miller

Cooking Clips

PICKLE BITES

"Simple, but very tasty appetizer"

8 oz. cream cheese
2 tbsp. minced onion
Small amount of mayonnaise
8 Clausen Dill pickle spears
16 pieces wheat bread

Mix first three ingredients together in small bowl. Cut 8 Clausen Dill pickle spears in half-lengthwise. Cut the crust off of 16 pieces of wheat bread. Spread with cream cheese mixture. Place one piece of pickle across bread and roll up. Cover with a damp cloth and refrigerate over night. Slice into small slices and serve.

Submitted by - Bruce Keeney

SPICY CHEESE STRAWS

Makes about 100 cheese straws

1 cup butter, melted
1 cup pecan pieces
1 tbsp. Creole seasoning salt
1 tsp. cayenne (pepper)
16 oz. extra-sharp cheddar, grated
2 cups all-purpose flour
1 tsp. baking powder

Preheat oven to 350°. Mix butter, pecans, seasoning salt and cayenne pepper in a large bowl. Add cheese and stir until well mixed. Add flour and baking powder a little at a time until all is incorporated. Form round wafers by placing ½ tbsp. of the mixture on foil-covered cookie sheets and flattening slightly. Bake for 20 to 25 minutes. Cool slightly before removing from foil.

Submitted by - JoAnn Pulliam, Office of U.S. Senator, Jim Webb

Cooking Clips

BROCCOLI SALAD

1 cup mayonnaise
½ cup sugar
½ cup vinegar
1 cup dried cranberries
½ cup shelled sunflower seeds
½ cup chopped purple onion
4 cups broccoli florets

Mix together and let chill overnight stirring several times.

Cooking Clips

Thayer Wine's Lime Shrimp Salad

1½ lbs. boiling potatoes
1/3 cup oil
¼ cup fresh lime juice
¼ cup minced parsley
½ tsp. salt
¼ tsp. pepper
¼ tsp. grated lime peel
Dash of sugar
2 tbsp. green onion
1 lb. unpeeled, raw shrimp (or ¾ pound cooked shrimp)
Lettuce leaves
1 avocado
1 tomato, cut into wedges
Watercress sprigs
Lime wedges

1 Cook potatoes in boiling water to cover about 30 minutes or until tender.

2 Combine oil, lime juice, parsley, salt, pepper, lime peel, and sugar; mix well. Peel and cut potatoes into ¼-inch slices; toss with onion. Pour about 1/3 cup lime marinade over warm potatoes; toss gently. Marinate 2 hours.

3 To cook raw shrimp, drop shrimp into boiling water; reduce heat and simmer 3 minutes or until lightly cooked and bright pink. Drain, peel, and devein if necessary.

4 Toss shrimp with about 3 tablespoons of lime marinade; marinate in refrigerator 2 hours.

5 Mound potato mixture on lettuce-lined platter. Slice avocado and dip in lime marinade. Arrange shrimp, avocado, and tomatoes around potatoes. Drizzle with remaining marinade. Garnish with watercress and lime wedges.

Cooking Clips

BIRD LEG

1 block Phillip cream cheese
1 small pkg. stick pretzels
1 pack chip beef

Let cheese warm until easy to spread on chip beef. Lay pretzel ½ in & ½ out. Quick and easy hors d'oeuvres.

Submitted by - Buddy Crowder
A dish he cooked for his kids when they were little.

ENTREES

Cooking Clips

CHICKEN ENCHILADAS

1 can cream of mushroom soup
1 can cream of chicken soup
(I also use creamy chicken mushroom)
1 cup evaporated milk
1 large onion (chopped)
1 stick margarine
2 jalapeños (seeded & diced)
1 pkg. Monterey jack cheese (grated)
(I use Monterey jack with jalapeño peppers.)
1 pkg. flour tortillas
1 small can chicken or leftover chicken or turkey

Sauté onion in butter. Add the two soups, milk, chicken and jalapeños. Heat until hot.

Place a large spoonful of mixture in center of each tortilla and roll up. Place in buttered casserole dish. Do this until you have about ¾ cup of mixture left. Spoon that over tortillas in pan and cover with Monterey jack.

I often double the recipe and make two layers, which serves about eight.

Submitted by-Tom & Linda Koertge

BAR-B-QUE CHICKEN

½ cup vegetable oil
1 cup vinegar
¼ cup water
2 tbsp. garlic powder
½ tsp. black ground pepper
1 tsp. crushed red peppers
½ tsp. chili powder
1 tsp. poultry seasoning
Few dashes of Texas Pete

Mix in quart jar with lid and shake well.
Marinate 24 hours or less if in a hurry, more if you have time.
Cook on grill basting and turning every 5 minutes or so till done.

Submitted by-Tom Wadkins
Major-Richmond City Sheriff's office (Retired)
AKA: Lanny's Cousin

Cooking Clips

CHUNKY TURKEY CHILI

Ground turkey, brightly colored vegetables and assertive seasonings combine for a super low calorie and great tasting meal. This recipe can be frozen

1 large onion, coarsely chopped	1 can (16 oz.) pinto beans or kidney beans, rinsed and drained
2 garlic cloves, minced	1 cup Pace Picante sauce
2 tsp. of olive oil	1 tbsp. beef flavored bouillon granules
1 lb. ground turkey	
1 ½ tsp. ground cumin	1 medium green bell pepper, cut into ¾ inch pieces
1 ½ tsp. chili powder	
1 can (28 oz) white tomatoes un-drained and coarsely chopped	1 medium red bell pepper, cut into ¾ inch pieces

Cook onion and garlic in oil in 12 inch skillet until tender, about 4 minutes. Add turkey; sprinkle with cumin and chili powder. Cook until no longer pink. Add tomatoes, Pace Picante Sauce and bouillon granules. Simmer uncovered 10 minutes. Add peppers; continue to simmer 10 minutes. Serve with additional Pace Picante Sauce. Makes eight 1-cup servings.

Submitted by-Hardman Jones and friends from the Federal Reserve Bank of Richmond

Cooking Clips

STUFFING FOR WILD DUCK

(Sufficient for two ducks or one wild goose.)

½ lb. hamburger
½ cup minced celery
½ cup minced onion
¼ cup minced green pepper
Bag of Catherine Clark's Sage Stuffing

Brown the hamburger. Do not pour off the fat. Add the vegetables and cook for several minutes and set aside.

In 3 cups of water cook the heart, the gizzard and the neck, with salt and pepper to taste and a bay leaf. Cool, remove the meat from the neck bone, and grind meat and giblets. Add them to the hamburger mixture. Add the package of sage dressing and as much of the liquid the giblets were cooked in to make a stuffing consistency.

Leftover dressing may be frozen for future use. This recipe may be used for domestic duck and goose as well.

If the birds are to be frozen, wrap them in moisture-proof material and freeze promptly. Don't freeze birds without plucking and cleaning them first or they may spoil or develop an off-taste.

Frozen ducks or geese may be stored up to 9-10 months. To thaw, place the package in the refrigerator for 12 to 18 hours. This slow thawing process helps tenderize the meat, according to food specialists.

Submitted by-Charlene K. Boynton

Cooking Clips

REMINGTON MALLARDS

Place ducks in pan breast up. Sprinkle each duck with one tablespoon of cooking sherry. Season each with:

½ tsp. celery salt
½ tsp. onion salt
½ tsp. celery seed
¼ teaspoon curry powder
1 tsp. salt
¼ tsp. pepper

Let stand in pan ½ to 1 hour

Chop 1 small onion and I stalk celery and place in pan. Add ¼ to ½ inch water. Bake at 500 degrees. until breast is brown (about 20 minutes). Turn and bake until back is brown. Cover and cook one hour at 300 degrees. Total cooking time, about 2 hours. If stuffing is desired, use any favorite poultry stuffing recipe (mouth-watering recipe).

Submitted by-Charlene K. Boynton

SMOKEHOUSE SPAGHETTI

¾ lb. spaghetti
½ lb. bacon
1 onion diced
1 ½-2 lbs. ground beef
2 8-oz. cans tomato sauce
1/8 tsp. pepper

½ tsp. oregano
½ tsp. garlic salt
1 can mushrooms
¼- ½ lb. shredded cheddar cheese
1 ½ tsp. salt

Sauté bacon, drain fat. Add onion and ground beef-brown and drain fat. Stir in tomato sauce, salt, pepper, oregano, garlic salt and mushrooms with liquid. Simmer 15 minutes. (May add a little Liquid Smoke.)

Cook spaghetti and drain. Stir into sauce. Place ½ of mixture into buttered 2 qt. dish. Top with ½ of each cheese. Repeat layers, but save a little of spaghetti mixture for last.

Bake 375 degrees for 20-25 minutes

Submitted by-Ken and Mary Stevens
(This has been in our family for over 50 years.)

FAVORITE CHILI

1 lb. extra lean ground beef
1 green pepper, chopped
1 medium onion, chopped
2 garlic cloves, minced
2 cans (14.5 oz.) Mexican style steamed tomatoes
1 can (16 oz.) chili beans
½ small butternut squash, peeled and cubed (about ½ cup)
(Can buy squash already cut up at some grocery stores)
1 cup of low sodium beef broth
1 ½ teaspoons ground cumin
1 ½ teaspoons chili powder
1 cup of frozen corn kernels

Cook first four ingredients in oven at medium heat until meat is no longer pink. Drain well and return to Dutch oven. Stir in tomatoes, chili beans, butternut squash, beef broth and spices. Bring to boil. Cover Dutch oven and reduce heat to medium low. Simmer, stir occasionally for 15 minutes. Stir in corn and cook uncovered for 15 minutes, or until squash is tender or chili done.

Submitted by-Jan & Dan Balfour

Cooking Clips

SLOW COOKER CRANBERRY ORANGE PORK LOIN

2 tbsp. olive oil
3 pounds pork loin roast, tied
½ tsp. salt
½ tsp. freshly ground black pepper
1 large sweet onion, coarsely chopped
2 cans (16 ounces each) whole-berry cranberry sauce
Grated zest of 2 oranges
Juice of 2 oranges (about 1 cup)
2 tsp. dried thyme leaves
½ cup beef broth

Spray the insert of a slow cooker with nonstick cooking spray.
Heat oil in large skillet over high heat. Sprinkle the roast with salt and pepper and add to pan.
Cook pork 2 minutes per side; transfer to slow cooker. Add onion, cranberry sauce, orange zest, and juice thyme and broth; stir.

Cover; cook pork on HIGH for 4 hours or on LOW for 8 hours.

Remove cover, transfer pork to cutting board and cover. Let rest for 15 minutes. Skim off fat from cooking liquid to make sauce.

Slice pork and serve with sauce.

Submitted by- George Hudgins

Cooking Clips

POTATO-SAUSAGE FOIL PACKS

1 package (14 oz.) smoked turkey kielbasa, sliced
2 large potatoes cut into wedges
1 each medium green, sweet red and yellow peppers, cut into 1-in pieces
1 medium onion, chopped
4 tsp. lemon juice
4 tsp. olive oil
½ tsp. garlic powder
½ tsp. pepper
¼ tsp. salt

Divide the kielbasa, potatoes, peppers, and onion among four double thicknesses of heavy-duty foil (about 18" x 12")
Drizzle with lemon juice and oil.
Sprinkle with garlic powder.
Pepper and salt.

Fold foil around kielbasa mixture and seal tightly.
Grill, covered, over medium heat for 30-35 minutes or until potatoes are tender.

Open foil carefully to allow steam to escape.

Submitted by-George Hudgins

Cooking Clips

SHRIMP AND SAUSAGE CREOLE

1 lb. fresh or frozen large shrimp
4 oz. smoked turkey sausage, halved lengthwise and sliced
1 medium onion, chopped
1 medium green sweet pepper, cut into bite-size strips
1 14 ½ ounce can whole tomatoes, undrained, cut-up
3 cloves garlic, minced
1 tsp. salt-free Cajun or Creole seasoning
2 cups hot cooked brown or white rice

Thaw shrimp, if frozen.
Peel shrimp, leaving tails intact if desired. Devein shrimp. Rinse shrimp, pat dry with paper towels. Set aside.

In a 4-quart Dutch oven, cook sausage, onion, and sweet pepper over medium-high heat about 5 minutes or until onion is tender and begins to brown. Add undrained tomatoes, garlic, and Cajun seasoning; stir until combined. Bring to boiling; reduce heat. Simmer, uncovered, for 5 minutes.

Stir in shrimp. Return to boiling; reduce heat. Cover and simmer for 2 to 3 minutes more or until shrimp turn opaque. Serve with rice. Makes 4 (about 1 ¼ cup) serving.

Submitted by-George Hudgins

George Hudgins – "I believe I was one of Mr. Campbell's first customers, if not the first customer, when he can to the "JM." Since I come from Williamsburg, most of the time to just get a cut, someday I'm going to figure the number of miles over 42 years. Then, see if the two of us can get in *The Guinness World Book of Records* … for the most miles driven by an idiot to get a haircut.

The Shrimp and sausage creole is one of our favorites and should be a good fit for Campbell's Louisiana roots."

Cooking Clips

MY MEATLOAF

2 lbs. hamburger
2 green peppers
2 onions
2 eggs
2 cans tomato sauce
Oatmeal

Fuse salt and pepper and add to taste
Bake 400 degrees
Bake from 1-2 hours
Check every half hour

Submitted by-Barbara Kersey

LOVER'S LOAF

¾ cup ground beef
¼ cup chopped onions
1 egg

3 slices American cheese
½ tsp. salt
¼ tsp. pepper

In a mixing bowl, combine beef, onions and egg, using hands rinsed in cold water. Take one half of mixture, mold in large flat patty, and place it in ungreased medium size skillet. Layer on cheese slices, and top with second patty. Place the cold skillet on stove, and set heat to medium/high. Sprinkle pepper on top and cover. Cook to desired denseness.

Prep time-10 minutes, serves 2.

Submitted by-George T. Bryson

Cooking Clips

RON'S WORLD FAMOUS MEAT LOAF (In the neighborhood)

One pound Ukrops Meatloaf Mix –some veal & pork-cooks choice
One cup crushed tortilla chips-in freezer bag roll with rolling pin
One cup shredded Colby & Monterey Jack Cheese – 1 cup
2/3 cup medium salsa
¾ cup beef broth with one egg beaten in broth (cold beef broth) so you don't cook egg
½ envelope taco seasoning sauce
½ cup Progresso seasoned bread crumbs
½ Package Lipton beefy onion soup mix
One cup cut up celery
One cup bell pepper & onion (Total)

Put all dry ingredients in bowl and mix well..
Add to meat loaf mix. Keep mixing until mixture no longer looks like hamburger.
Add salsa and beef broth with egg. Mix well.
Cook celery, pepper and onion in fry pan with 1/3 stick of butter until partially cooked (soft). Add to meat mixture. Mix thoroughly.
Pack mixture into mixing bowl solid with spatula. Shape into loaf and put into baking dish. Slope sides to hold glaze.
Prepare glaze. Mix 1/3 cup brown sugar with 2/3 cup ketchup.
Add glaze before putting meatloaf in oven. Add glaze every 20 minutes.
Cook at 375 degrees for about one hour. Meat thermometer should read 160 degrees when done. Don't over cook.

OR

Make into small meatballs
Cook on cookie sheet in oven
Glaze after cooked
Put in crock pot & serve warm as hors d'oeuvres with toothpicks

"Do not put ketchup on this meatloaf"

Submitted anonymously

CHICKEN WITH DRIED BEEF

Ingredients:

1 jar dried beef, about 2 ½ oz., rinsed
6 boneless chicken breast halves, skin removed
6 slices bacon
¼ cup sour cream
¼ cup flour
1 can of mushroom soup, undiluted
2 to 3 tbsp. dry white wine, optional

Preparation:

On bottom of greased slow cooker, arrange dried beef. Wrap each piece of chicken with a strip of bacon; arrange on top of dried beef. In small bowl, combine sour cream and flour; add soup and wine, if using, and blend thoroughly. Pour over chicken mixture. Cover and cook on LOW for 6 to 8 hours. Serves 6.

Submitted by-Bill Overton

Cooking Clips

BILLY'S CHILI

This recipe was given to me by an elderly lady in St. Cloud, Florida over 30 years ago. I kept making changes until I found the taste both me and my family loves. Voted number one Chili by my wife and daughters-an important poll, no less.

2 lbs. stewing beef cut in ½" or smaller cubes
1 large sweet onion
1 clove of garlic

(Brown beef in frying pan and drain. Also, brown onion with garlic in frying pan, mix with beef and put in a large pot.)

Add In:

2 –15 oz cans of tomato sauce or one-28 oz. Ragu pasta sauce-w/mushroom & pepper.3-15 oz. cans of dark kidney beans
1 cup brown sugar
1 tbsp. cumin
2 tbsp. chili powder
2 bell peppers-chopped (red or yellow for 1 and 1 green)
1 tbsp. salt
2 tbsp. Worcestershire sauce

Add hot peppers to your taste (chopped jalapeño's and/or Tabasco)

Cook on low heat for 5-6 hours

Submit by-Bill Shurm: Varina-1963; VCU-1968

Cooking Clips

EGG & HERRING ROLL CASSEROLE

6 eggs
2 small cans herring roe

Drain herring roe
Casserole pan
Margarine or oil
Line pan with roe
Whip eggs & pour on top
Bake at 350 degrees until eggs rise and brown

Submitted by-Buddy Crowder

RAGU

This Neapolitan Sunday dish is excellent for a company dinner—easy to prepare and wonderful to eat.

1 pork loin (size according to number to be served)
1 28 oz. can tomato puree
1 can tomato paste
1 cup red wine (use your own judgment here)
Several cloves of garlic, minced
Salt and pepper to taste
Basil, parsley minced and oregano (use your own judgment)

Brown pork loin in olive oil to seal in juices. Add remaining ingredients. Simmer about 2 hours or until pork is done. Serve with ziti macaroni and grated cheese. With a fresh green salad, fruit dessert, good wine, crusty bread. This is a great meal.

Submitted by-Art Ritter

Cooking Clips

PASTA PUTTANESCA (Sauce of the Streetwalker)

9 medium fresh tomatoes or 1 can tomatoes (15 oz.)
2 tbsp. olive oil
1 large onion minced
3 tbsp. minced parsley
several cloves of garlic minced
½ cup sliced green olives
1 ½ tbsp. capers
1 can (2 oz.) anchovies, drained, minced-optional
1 lb. pasta (spaghetti or noodles) thin noodles or linguine

If fresh tomatoes are used, put in large container and cover with very hot water. Let sit for about 10 minutes...then peel, chop coarse and set aside.

In large sauce pan, heat olive oil and lightly brown onions, garlic and parsley (about 5 minutes). Add olives, capers, anchovies and tomatoes. Cover, bring to boil and simmer about 20 minutes.

Cook pasta; serve while hot with sauce; top with grated cheese if desired. Serves 6.

Submitted by-Art Ritter

These are recipes from my Mother-in-law. She lived in Italy for a while (not as a street walker) and got them there. She (Esther Acanfora) passed them on to my wife, Mary Ritter, and we enjoy both of them; the pasta for a quick and easy meal, the ragu for a special meal.

Cooking Clips

CHICKEN CASSEROLE

2 cups cooked chicken, cut into bite size pieces
½ cup mayonnaise
1 can mushroom soup
1 medium can pimento
½ cup grated sharp cheese
½ tsp. curry powder
1 can sliced water chestnuts
½ cup chopped parsley

Mix together and top with buttered breadcrumbs and sliced almonds

Bake at 325 degrees about 35 minutes or until bubbly.

Serves 6

Submitted by-Dallas Reid

Cooking Clips

CRISPY CHICKEN WITH ORANGE PEEL

4 tbsp. soy sauce
¾ cup white wine
2 cups cornstarch
2 oranges, peel only, cut into ¼ in. strips
¾ cup sugar
4 egg whites
2 tbsp. white vinegar
6 dried red hot pepper (optional...or reduce quantity for a milder taste

2 tbsp. catsup
4 scallions including tops
20 snow peas, washed
8 chicken breast halves, boneless-cut in 1 inch chunks

1. Make sauce:

Mix sugar, vinegar, catsup, soy mix and wine in saucepan. Add hot peppers and simmer over medium heat until reduced to the consistency of syrup. As sauce thickens, watch closely so it does not caramelize.

2. Prepare chicken:

Separate egg whites and place in bowl. Place the cornstarch in another large bowl. Cut chicken into chunks about 1 inch wide by 1 ½ inches long. Dredge in egg white and then in cornstarch until well coated.

3. Deep fry chicken:

Fill wok, deep fryer, or large pot about half full of oil, preferably peanut oil. Heat oil to about 375 degrees. Working in batches suitable for fryer, deep fry the chicken and orange peel until light brown. Keep warm in a 200 degree oven until all the chicken is cooked.

4. Assemble:

Place fried chicken in large bowl. Add the sauce and mix well. Do not saturate the chicken with sauce. A light coating is ideal. Transfer the coated chicken to serving platter and garnish with thinly sliced scallions and snow peas. Serve at once!

Servings: 4

Continued, next page . . .

Cooking Clips

Tips: The sauce takes a while to reduce and can be prepared ahead of time if desired. Reheat before using.

It is important to heavily coat the chicken with cornstarch. This can also be done several hours in advance and refrigerated.

Do not overload the storage container if prepared in advance. This will cause the chicken to stick together.

Peel the oranges by scoring all the way around the orange with the point of a small knife. Rotate 90 degrees and score again.

Carefully separate peel from orange, then cut into ¼ inch strips.

This recipe makes generous servings....but it keeps well in the refrigerator and is also delicious cold.

Submitted by-Harold Burnley

Cooking Clips

HOT HAM BISCUITS

1 package of 20 rolls
8 slices Smithfield ham, thinly sliced
Grated or sliced swiss cheese (8 slices)

Mix:

1 stick butter (make sure it's softened, but not melted)
Grate ¼ of an onion
1 tbsp. Dijon mustard
Add poppy seeds

Slice the package of rolls in half; spread mixture on both sides of the rolls. Use 8 slices of thinly-sliced Smithfield ham and cover with Swiss cheese.

Bake at 325 degrees for 45 minutes

Submitted by-Robert Zehmer

Cooking Clips

VENISON ROAST

Brown roast in olive oil. Add unpeeled potatoes, quartered, carrots, onions, celery. Add 1 pkg. dry onion soup, 1 can cream mushroom soup, 1 can peeled whole tomatoes. Salt and pepper to taste, add several shakes Mrs. Dash. Cover and cook at 350 degrees for 2 ½ to 3 hours, depending on size of roast.

Submitted- Ed Rhodes

SWEET–N-SOUR KRAUT

1 (16-oz.) bag sauerkraut
1 cup water
1 apple, diced

1 tbsp. brown sugar
caraway seed, to taste
dillweed, to taste

Drain and rinse sauerkraut. Add water, apple, brown sugar, caraway seed and dill. Simmer 45 minutes. Taste to see if you need more sugar or herbs.

Note: Goes great with kielbasa, brats, pork and turkey.

Submitted by-Carol Rhodes

Cooking Clips

MARYLAND LUMP CRAB CAKES

Ingredients:

4 tbsp. mayonnaise
1 tsp. Old Bay Spice
1 tsp. mustard
½ tsp. Worcestershire Sauce
1 egg
3 slices diced white bread (crusts removed)
1 lb. backfin crab meat, shell removed

Mix mayonnaise, Old Bay spice, mustard, Worcestershire sauce, egg and bread. Fold in crab meat. Mold mixture into 8 patties. Place on buttered baking sheet.

Bake 12 minutes at 500 degrees

Submitted by-Bob Bledsoe

CRAB CAKES

Makes 6 hamburger sized cakes

1 lb. crab meat (Phillips), shells removed
2 heaping tablespoons mayo
2 eggs, slightly beaten
½ tsp. Worcestershire Sauce
½ tsp. cayenne pepper
¼ tsp. salt
½ small onion-grated
½ tbsp. mustard powder
18 Ritz crackers, crumbled

Combine all ingredients except crackers. Add crackers in close to sautéing as possible. Won't get moist.
Form into patties size of hamburger. Sauté in frying pan on medium high in butter. 10 min. side

Submitted by-Rowland George

ARGENTINE SHEPHERDS PIE

Serves 4-5 persons
2 lbs. minced beef
1 large onion, chopped
1 clove garlic
Beef stock
Bay leaf
1 ½-2 tbsp of ground cumin
chili powder
2.0 oz. Sultanas (white raisins)
Salt/pepper
Sliced olives optional (green)
Oil

Fry onions in oil until soft, add crushed garlic. Stir, add beef slowly and brown all over. Add cumin, salt, bay leaf and chili powder. Mixed thoroughly over moderate heat. Add ¼-1/2 pt. of beef stock. (enough to cover) Add Sultanas and leave to simmer 45 min to hour, add chopped onions, olives and leave to cool for 5 minutes. Put into casserole dish and cover with layer of mashed potato. Dot with butter and grill until brown.

Given to me by a cousin from Argentina one Christmas in England.

Submitted by-Malcolm Warneford-Thomson

Cooking Clips

CHICKEN PARMIGIANA

4 boneless chicken breasts (medium sized-not too big)
Seasoned flour (with pepper and salt, etc. to taste)
2 eggs, beaten
Italian bread crumbs with some Parmesan cheese mixed in (to taste)
Olive oil
Prepared red sauce (your favorite spaghetti sauce)
½ lb. mozzarella cheese slices
½ cup grated Parmesan cheese

Place chicken breast between sheets of wax paper and pound or roll thin.
Dip chicken in seasoned flour to coat, then in beaten egg, and then coat with breadcrumbs mixture.
In large skillet, quickly sauté chicken in hot oil until golden brown on both sides. Drain on paper towels.
Arrange chicken in shallow baking dish. Cover with red sauce. Place mozzarella cheese slice on top of each chicken breast.
Sprinkle with Parmasen cheese and bake at 350° for 15 minutes until bubbly.

Serve as is or over rice or pasta.

(Recipe can easily be adjusted for different serving amounts)

Submitted by - Ron Rash
from Anita

Cooking Clips

CHICKEN DIVAN

"I'm not a very big fan of chicken, but this recipe is downright tasty. This recipe make 3-4 servings, so don't be afraid to double it."

Ingredients:
1 pkg. boneless/skinless chicken breasts
1 pkg. frozen broccoli (preferred florets)
1 can cream of chicken soup
½ cup mayonnaise
1 tbsp. lemon juice
½ cup shredded cheese

Directions:
1. Rinse and boil the chicken breasts for 20 minutes. Remove and let them cool to the point where you can cut the chicken up into small pieces.
2. Layer the Broccoli onto the bottom of glass baking dish.
3. Layer the small pieces of chicken breast on top of broccoli.
4. In a separate bowl, mix cream of chicken soup, mayonnaise, lemon juice, and cheddar cheese. (Make sure mixture covers the entire top. If you don't, any uncovered portions will be rubbery and somewhat unpleasant to eat.)
5. Bake at 350° for 45 minutes.

My John Marshall Barber Shop moment:

"As a middle school and high school teacher, each fall invariably means homecoming, and homecoming wouldn't be complete without spirit week. For spirit week, students and staff are encouraged to show school spirit by dressing for spirit days, such as mismatch day, school colors day, or - at least in this particular case – twin day.

For twin day two years ago, a female colleague and I were twins: we both wore black pants, a white button-down shirt, and a red tie. This year when twin day rolled around, my twin happened to be pregnant. Not one to shy away from a good laugh (and since I have a somewhat suspect sense of humor), I agreed to dress up as twins again this year, but this time we wore a matching maternity shirt (mine stuffed with a pillow), black pants and a long black wig. Needless to say, my coworkers and students were caught off guard. Even more than that,

Continued, next page . . .

many of them did not quite know what to make of the whole deal, particularly my female coworkers and students. Given that I'm about 6'3" and over 200 pounds, I can see how this might have looked a little bizarre.

As Luck would have it, twin day was also the day I had scheduled to get my haircut. It was a hot day, and on my way to the barber shop I was glad to be done with the whole deal, particularly the wig. As I got closer to the barber shop and thought about it, I thought it would be a shame to go to all of that trouble and not let everyone in the barber shop have a little fun with it, and for the most part they did. Mr. Campbell and Ebony nearly split their side laughing once they went from their initial confusion to understanding what was going on. All of us had a pretty good laugh with it.

All of us, that is, except for another customer in the barber shop. He clearly did not know what to do with it, but what he did know was that he didn't like it. He didn't like it at all. Even once I had taken the wig off and talked about twin day and spirit week, he was still obviously uncomfortable. I'm sure if you talked to him now, he would try to downplay it, but make no mistake about it, my spirit wear was getting the better of him.

When I look back at it now, I'm not sure which part I like better. On one hand, I really enjoyed the initial look of confusion from Mr. Campbell and Ebony. On the other, it really kind of amuses me how uncomfortable the other customer was. In the end I don't have to settle. I just enjoy them both for what they are."

Submitted by - John Andrews

Cooking Clips

CRAB MEAT CASSEROLE

1 lb. lump crabmeat (pick through and remove any shells)
1 cup mayonnaise
1 tbsp. Durkees Famous Sauce
1 tbsp. Worcestershire sauce
2 eggs, well beaten
Salt & pepper
1 tbsp. butter, melted

Add all ingredients except butter and lightly mix, (try not to break up crabmeat chunks) put into a greased casserole dish, pour butter over top and bake in 350° oven for 30-40 minutes. Serves 4. If you want to turn this into a dip for bread or crackers, add 1 bar of cream cheese.

Submitted by - G. Olin Hardy, IV   Recipe from Anne Hardy

POTATO CHEESE CASSEROLE

32 oz. frozen hash browns, loose kind
2 pkgs. French onion dip (8 oz. each)
2 cups shredded sharp cheddar cheese or Velveeta cheese
1 stick (1/2 cup) margarine, melted
1 can cream of chicken soup

Mix well. Place in large casserole dish. Sprinkle with paprika.

Topping:
1 stick (1/2 cup) margarine, melted
2 cups corn flakes

Mix and top casserole. Bake at 350° for one hour.

Submitted by - Tom and Jeanne Hughes

Cooking Clips

GRAMMA KRUSE'S ITALIAN SPAGHETTI

SAUCE:
36 oz. tomato paste (not sauce)
36 oz. water
2½ tsp. sugar
1¼ tsp. salt
Garlic (cut up cloves of fresh or use powder)
1½ tsp. crushed red pepper

MEATBALLS:
1½ lbs. lean hamburger
Garlic (same as above)
3 eggs
2 tsp. sugar
2 tsp. salt
2 tsp. crushed red pepper
Cracker meal

SAUCE: Mix and let heat up slowly

MEATBALLS: Mix well, then add ¼ to ½ box cracker meal, or enough to make firm. Form into small meatballs, brown slowly and lightly in buttered frying pan, turning to brown all over. Put meatballs into sauce and simmer slowly for at least 4-5 hours. Better if made a day ahead of time.

SPAGHETTI: Cook 1 ½ pounds long, thin spaghetti into boiling, salted water to al dente. Pour sauce with meatballs over it. Serve with freshly grated Parmesan cheese.

Submitted by – A Loyal Customer

Cooking Clips

WESTERN BAKED BEANS

2 lbs. or more pork and beans
1 cup ketchup
2 tbsp. vinegar
2 tbsp. mustard
1 lb. ground beef
1 pkg. Lipton dry onion soup mix

Brown beef; drain. Mix in all other ingredients. Bake in 325° oven for one hour.

Tips: Recipe can easily be doubled. Can make ahead, refrigerate and bake whenever.

"Guys love this – it is a very hearty/bold dish – gets better with each serving!! (Warms over well.)"

Submitted by – Bev Beadles

HUSBAND'S DELIGHT

1 lb. ground round beef
2 small cans tomato sauce
1 (8 oz.) block cream cheese
2 pkgs. grated sharp cheddar cheese
1 small sour cream (8 oz.)
1 bag slim noodles (spaghetti/egg/fettucini, lasagna, etc.)

Bake at 325° for 20-25 minutes, until bubbly and brown. Brown meat, seasoned with garlic and onion. Pour in tomato sauce, mix and simmer. Cook noodles according to package; drain. Combine cream cheese and sour cream together.
In 11" x 7" casserole dish –
Assemble in this order:
First: layer of noodles
Second: meat mixture
Third: sour cream mixture
Fourth: top with grated cheese.

(Repeat layers until finished.)

Submitted by - Bev Hollingsworth

Cooking Clips

CHICKEN WITH TOMATOES AND FETA

Makes 4 servings

1 tsp. oil
4 small boneless skinless chicken breast halves (1 lb.)
1 onion, chopped
1 can (14-1/2oz.) Italian-style diced tomatoes, undrained
¼ cup light Greek or balsamic vinaigrette dressing
1 lemon, thinly sliced
½ cup Crumbled Feta cheese with Basil and tomato

Heat oil in large skillet on medium-high heat. Add chicken and onions; cover. Cook 10 to 14 min. or until chicken is done (165°), turning after 6 min. Remove chicken from skillet; cover to keep warm. Add tomatoes, dressing, and lemons to onions in skillet' cook 4 min. or until heated through, stirring frequently. Return chicken to skillet. Spoon sauce over chicken. Cook one min. or until chicken is heated through; top with cheese.

Submitted by - Connie Sorrell via the Zacharias Ganey Health Institute

Cooking Clips

BARBECUE (NORTH CAROLINA STYLE)

5 lb. pork shoulder (bone-in or boneless)
Red pepper
16 oz. apple cider vinegar
Sauer's brand mild or hot barbecue sauce

Coat both sides of pork with red pepper. Place in deep roasting pan. Pour all of 16 oz. apple cider vinegar over pork. Tent loosely with foil. Cook at 325° for eight hours. Remove from oven; discard liquid. Remove bone and fat from meat. Pull pork into small pieces. Season with Sauer's mild or hot barbeque sauce. Cook as directed, and you will love it. Enjoy.

Submitted by - Bill and Bev McGhee

WONDERFUL WHITE CHILI

1 lb. dry white beans, rinsed and soaked overnight
6 cups chicken broth
2 onions, chopped
1 tbsp. oil
6-8 cloves minced garlic
3 oz. diced green chilies
4 tsp. ground cumin
2 tsp. dried oregano
3 tsp. cayenne pepper
4 cups cooked chicken, diced
1 cup sour cream
3 cups shredded Monterey Jack cheese

Combine beans and broth in large pot. Simmer for two hours. Sauté onions in oil until golden. Add everything else to bean mixture except last two ingredients and simmer for two more hours. Add sour cream and cheese at the end. Heat until cheese melts. You may garnish with chopped cilantro, green onions, tomatoes, and cheese. Not suitable for freezing. Serves 10.

Submitted by - JoAnn Pulliam, Office of U.S. Senator, Jim Webb

Cooking Clips

ASPARAGUS AND CHICKEN CASSEROLE

2 cups cooked chicken
1 can asparagus
1 can cream of mushroom soup
1 can cream of chicken soup
1 cup sour cream
Butter bread crumbs

Layer a two-quart casserole dish with chicken and asparagus. Mix the cream of mushroom and chicken soups together with the sour cream, and spread onto asparagus. Top with buttered breadcrumbs. Bake at 350° for 45-50 minutes.

Enjoy.

Submitted by - Sharon and Hugh Campbell

GRILLED OR BAKED SALMON WITH HONEY MUSTARD DILL SAUCE OR DILL CUCUMBER SAUCE

Serves 3 - 4 (about 4oz. - 6oz. per person)

Whole side of fish, wild salmon
½ cup soy sauce

Marinate fish for 30 minutes in soy sauce.
Preheat oven to 500° or grill to 450-500°.

To bake: place in an oil-coated baking pan.
To grill: coat the grill with oil before placing fish on grill, skin side up first for just a few minutes.

Finish by turning fish over to have skin side cook last.
Bake or grill approximately 8 to 10 minutes or until fish is firm/done.
Serve with either of the two following sauces.
For company, serve both! Also great with smoked salmon!

Submitted by - Ray and Connie Sorrell

Cooking Clips

PESTO ROAST BEEF PANINI

Bread (Italian)
Deli Roast Beef
Pesto Mix
Mozzarella cheese
Butter

Spread Pesto on two slices of bread. Add roast beef and cheese. Put slices together. In pan, fry both sides of bread with butter - like a grilled cheese sandwich. Serve hot with fries or chips.

Submitted by - "Marielle"

CHESAPEAKE CRAB CASSEROLE

Ingredients:

1 lb. backfin lump Crabmeat
½ lb. medium shrimp
1 can Campbell's Cream of Celery soup
1 large egg
1 tsp. each of Worcestershire Sauce, lemon juice, parsley flakes, Phillips Seafood Seasoning, hot/sweet mustard & black pepper
¼ tsp. Coleman's dry mustard
1 heaping tbsp. Miracle Whip mayonnaise
4 slices of fresh white bakery bread without crusts
4 oz. of Asiago cheese

Combine in small mixing bowl the egg, Worcestershire Sauce, lemon juice, parsley flakes, dry mustard, hot/sweet mustard, Phillips Seafood Seasoning, mayonnaise, black pepper and Cream of Celery Soup.

Lightly mix crabmeat, broken pieces of bread and 3 ounces of grated Asiago cheese in large bowl. Pour in ingredients from small mixing bowl, add shrimp and mix ingredients thoroughly. Place in 9"x9" Pyrex baking dish and cook for 50-60 minutes at 350°. Sprinkle 1 ounce of Asiago cheese on top and allow casserole to lightly brown.

Cooking Clips

CYBER CHILI
Y2K Compliant

Developed for the family, friends and guests of
Dick Parkinson

Compliant Ingredients:

1 lb. lean ground beef
1.5 lbs. of stew beef (or beef tenderloin), cut up into small, bite size pieces
4 large onions, chopped
2 cloves garlic (minced)
2 cups barbecue sauce (with hickory & brown sugar if available)
1 cup water (may substitute a medium dry red wine)
1 tbsp. chili powder
1 tsp. ground black pepper
1 oz. unsweetened chocolate, grated
1 tsp. *each*: ground cumin, turmeric, allspice, cinnamon
1/4 tsp. *each:* coriander, cardamom
1 tsp. salt
2 cups fresh, sliced mushrooms and 2 cups whole (button size) mushrooms
2 (16-oz.) cans each of dark red kidney beans, Great Northern beans & chili beans
2 oz. sliced pimientos
3 (14.5-oz.) cans of diced tomatoes
tomato juice, as needed
8 oz. *each:* Wisconsin Sharp Cheddar, Vermont White Cheddar, Monterey Jack Natural Cheese, grated

The essence:
Preheat 8 qt stainless steel pot on low to medium heat. Add meat, break up with fork and cook until lightly browned. Drain off fat. Add water, barbecue sauce, diced tomatoes, onions, garlic, mushrooms, pimientos, and kidney beans. Bring to boil. Add chili powder, black pepper, garlic, chocolate, cumin, turmeric, allspice, salt, cinnamon, coriander and cardamom. Cover and simmer on VERY LOW HEAT for 2.5 to 3 hours. Stir and taste occasionally (can you resist it?) and add tomato juice if it gets too dry to ladle up easily. Serve in Y2k Compliant bread boule (a round, half-pound loaf of sourdough bread with the top sliced off and the inside scooped out to make room for the Cyber Chili. Sprinkle grated cheeses on top. RECIPE SERVES 10 - 12 CYBER TECHIES.

Cooking Clips

ORANGE CHICKEN

3 Boneless, skinless chicken breasts
1 Stick salted butter (¼ lb.)
3 to 4 Cloves fresh garlic
1 (4.5 oz.) can sliced mushrooms
1 container frozen orange juice concentrate
½ gal. Lots of Pulp Tropacana orange juice
White Rice (Enough for 3 to 6 servings, see below)

I prefer to use an electric skillet.
In skillet, melt butter on very low heat. Add chopped garlic, mushrooms and sliced water chestnuts. Simmer in butter stirring frequently until garlic and other ingredients are tender. Be very careful not to scorch. Place chicken into ingredients and slowly cook, turning frequently, until each side of chicken begins to very lightly brown.
Add frozen orange juice concentrate and slowly cook for about 10 minutes after completely thawed. Add "Lots of Pulp Tropacana" orange juice, enough to all but cover the chicken breasts. Heat can be increased to a level to cook more vigorously. Leaving the lid off of the electric skillet while cooking will tend to make juice thicker, which I like better; however, you will have to add more juice at some point. Periodically, check chicken breast with fork or knife to determine when cooked through. Chicken breasts may be divided for additional servings. Serve over cooked rice and enjoy! Leftovers, if any, are great the next day or so.

Submitted by - Larry Davidson
Cumberland, Va.
John Marshall Barber Shop haircuts since 1966.

Cooking Clips

PAKISTANI SEEKH KABAB

Ingredients:
1 lb ground beef
1 medium onion chopped
2 serrano peppers chopped
1/2 tsp. paprika
1/2 tsp. red chilli powder
1 tsp leveled salt
1 egg
1/4 bunch chopped cilantro

Directions:
Mix above ingredients and shape like hot dogs. Cook on griddle or frying pan medium-high heat for approximately 15 minutes.
Eat with Tandoori naan (available at Indian grocery stores).

Submitted by- Nadeem Miza

Cooking Clips

CREOLE BEEF STEW

2 lbs. beef stew meat
1/3 cup flour
3½ tsp. salt
½ tsp. black pepper
2 tbsp. shortening
1 cup water
1 cup onions, sliced
1 cup sliced fresh or frozen pack of okra
1 cup fresh corn, cut from the cob
1 cup potatoes, diced
2 cups (1 pound) tomatoes, canned
¼ tsp. instant minced garlic
½ tsp. chili powder (or to the taste)

Trim off and discard excess fat from the meat. Cut beef into 1-inch cubes. Mix flour with salt and black pepper, and sprinkle over the meat. Mix well. Brown on all sides in shortening. Add water. Cover and simmer 1½ to 2 hours or until meat is tender. Add remaining ingredients 30 minutes before cooking time is up. Serve hot.

Submitted by – Jack Spiro: "A recipe from my hometown (and Sharon's country, too.)"

Cooking Clips

SHRIMP BOIL

1/3 cup Old Bay Seasoning
2 bags small red potatoes
2 Hillshire reduced fat smoked sausages
8 ears corn (broken in half)
3-4 lbs. shrimp (leave shells on)

Fill large pot halfway with water and bring to boil
Add potatoes and reduce heat for gentle boil-cook for 30 minutes
Add Old Bay Seasoning
Add sausage-cook 10 minutes
Add corn-cook 5 minutes
Drain water
Slice sausage into ½ inch slices
Present all ingredients on warm platter
Serve with ice-cold beer!
Feeds 8-10 hearty appetites

Submitted by -Scott and Kathe Hetzer
Campbell's customer since circa 1972

GEORGE ALLEN'S FAVORITE LASAGNA RECIPE

Sauce:
1 tbsp. olive oil
1 large onion, finely chopped
1 large garlic clove, minced
2 (28 oz.) can tomatoes, coarsely chopped
1 (12 oz.) can tomato paste
1 (12 oz.) can water
1 tbsp. oregano
1 ½ tbsp. basin
1 bay leaf
1 tsp. garlic powder
2 tsp. sugar
1 ½ tsp. salt
Black pepper to taste
*Sauté onions and garlic until transparent in olive oil
*Combine remaining ingredients; simmer several hours until smooth and thick.

Lasagna:
1 (16oz.) box lasagna, parboiled and drained
Olive oil
1 large onion, chopped
1 clove garlic, minced
1 ½ lbs. ground beef
1 ½ lbs. Italian sausage
1 lb. mushrooms, sliced
½ lb. mozzarella cheese, grated
½ cup Parmesan cheese
2 eggs, beaten
Salt & pepper to taste
Sauté onions in small amount of olive oil. Add garlic.
- Brown ground beef, sausage and mushrooms. Cool mixture.

Continued . . .

Cooking Clips

- Preheat oven to 350 degrees.
- Spread small amount of sauce in bottom of 9' x 13' pan. Line with lasagna. Layer half the meat mixture, 1/3 the sauce, and 1/3 the combination of chesses. Repeat layering with lasagna, meat, sauce, and cheese. Place remaining lasagna on top. Spread with sauce and cheese
- Bake one hour

Some time ago Hugh had a wonderful assistant barber from Poland who would cut my hair. One time when she was using scissors, I mistakenly heard her say to me, "You have sick hair."

I stayed quiet for a minute or two wondering how my hair could be ailing.

After a while I asked her how my hair could be ill. How did she diagnose such a malady?

After some back and forth translating, I was happy to finally understand that she said I had "thick" hair, and I breathed a sigh of relief. Thick hair is good.

The lesson is while at the John Marshall Barbershop with shears buzzing and scissors cutting, listen closely. With Hugh and all the folks in that historic barbershop, one will get more than a great haircut. One can get good common-sense wisdom and memorable humor.

– George Allen

ALMA'S WHITE BEAN CHICKEN CHILI

2-15 ½ oz. cans Cannellini beans, un-drained or Great Northern beans, un drained)
1-14 ½ oz. can diced tomatoes, DRAINED (Alma uses Del Monte w/zest, mild green chilies)
2- cooked chicken breasts cut into ½ inch, pieces
1-package McCormick White Chicken Chili seasoning mix
1-cup water
1/3 cup diced onions
1/3 cup diced green bell pepper
1/3 cup diced yellow pepper
1/3 cup diced red pepper

Put all the ingredients into a large pot and bring to a boil. Cover, reduce heat and simmer on medium-low heat being careful not to scorch beans.
Chili can be ready to serve in about 30 minutes, however, the longer it cooks, the better it tastes. Try cooking today, refrigerating overnight, then reheating and serving tomorrow-a real treat.

Submitted-P.J. and Alma Smith

Cooking Clips

COTTAGE PIE

1 roll ground beef
½ container beef base
1 cup A1 sauce
6 large carrots, diced
1 tbsp. garlic powder

Break ground beef up into small pieces, cover with water and add carrots, garlic and beef base. Bring to a boil, reduce heat and simmer until meat is cooked through. Cool cottage pie in ice bath in sink. Fat will harden on top. SCOOP Off hardened fat and drain off water. Mix in A1 sauce and store.

Submitted by-Terry Rose Oneill
Penny Lane Pub

SIDES

Cooking Clips

SQUASH PUDDING

Slice about 8 to 10 very small, yellow squash and boil until tender. Mash, add salt and 2 tbsp. of butter. Beat 2 eggs and add 2 Tbsp. sugar, 1 Tbsp. flour. To this mixture, add 2 cups milk and then blend (a blender can be used to mix completely) into the cooked squash. Flavor with the juice of a half lemon. Place in a baking dish and dot with butter. Bake at 325° for 45 minutes.

Submitted by - Tom and Jeanne Hughes

Cooking Clips

HOT POLISH POTATO SALAD

1 loop of Kielbasa sausage, sliced ¼" thick
1 large onion, peeled and chopped
1 tbsp. butter
½ cup sour cream
¼ cup mayonnaise
2 tbsp. yellow mustard
2 large cans of sliced potatoes, drained and rinsed
Pepper to taste

Brown sausage and onion in butter. Stir in mayonnaise, sour cream, and mustard until smooth. Add potatoes and stir lightly until potatoes are coated. Add pepper. Serve hot.

Submitted by - Ronald W. Davis, Church Hill (VA)

Cooking Clips

SPINACH-STUFFED SQUASH

4 large yellow squash
2 (10 oz.) packages frozen chopped spinach
1/3 cup butter or margarine
1/3 cup chopped onion
1 (3 oz.) package cream cheese, cubed
1 tsp. garlic salt
½ tsp. ground black pepper (I don't like a lot of pepper so I used only ¼ tsp.)
1/8 tsp. ground red pepper (I use a pinch)
¼ cup grated Parmesan cheese
2 tbsp. fine, dry breadcrumbs (I combined the crumbs and cheese together before sprinkling on squash)

Wash, then cook whole squash in boiling water to cover 10 minutes or until crisp-tender; drain and cool. Cut squash in half lengthwise; remove and discard seeds. Place shells in a lightly greased 13 x 9 inch pan.
Cook spinach according to package directions; drain well, pressing between layers of paper towels.
Melt butter in a large skillet; add onion, and sauté until tender. Add spinach, cream cheese, and next 3 ingredients, stirring until cheese melts; spoon evenly into squash shells. Sprinkle with Parmesan cheese and breadcrumbs. Bake at 400 degrees for 20 minutes, or until thoroughly heated.

Submitted by-Jerry Lindquist

Cooking Clips

CORN PUDDING

1 can cream style yellow corn
1 can white Shoepeg corn
3 eggs
¾ cup sugar
1 tbsp. flour
½ stick butter
2 tbsp. milk
Nutmeg (optional)

Mix eggs (well beaten), sugar, flour together and add corn. Then add milk, slice butter on top, sprinkle nutmeg and bake at 325 degrees for 45 minutes.

Submitted by-Carol & Jesse Romer

Cooking Clips

BAKED BRIE IN FILO CUPS

30 mini Filo-dough cups
Brie cheese cut in ½ inch cube without rind
Apricot jam
Chopped almonds

Put ½ tsp. jam in each Filo cup. Top with ½ cube of Brie cheese. Add small amount of chopped almonds on top of cheese. Bake on parchment lined sheet for 15 minutes at 350 degrees.

Submitted by-Ed Southward

"NEVER FAIL" CORN PUDDING

4 ears white corn (can use similar amount of frozen shoepeg white corn)
4 ½ tsp. sugar
Pepper
3 tbsp. flour
2 eggs, beaten
½ tsp. salt
2 tbsp. butter, melted
1 ½ cups milk

Cut corn off cob, scraping ears well. Add sugar, flour, salt and pepper. Blend in beaten egg, butter and milk.

Bake in uncovered greased Pyrex casserole at 350 degrees in preheated oven. Serves 4-5.

(Used in my family for 3 generations, some varying amounts of ingredients slightly to taste. ENJOY this easy recipe!)

Submitted by-R. Garnett Hall, Jr. - & family

BREAD

EPSTEIN FAMILY PUMPKIN BREAD

Ingredients:
- 3 cups sugar
- 1 one lb. can of pumpkin
- 2/3 cup water
- 1 tsp. baking powder
- 3 ½ cups all purpose flour
- ¼ tsp. ground clove
- ½ tsp. Allspice
- 1 cup vegetable oil
- 4 eggs
- ½ tsp. salt
- 2 tsp. Baking soda
- 1 tsp. cinnamon
- 1 tsp. nutmeg

Preheat oven to 350 degrees. Grease and flour a nonstick angel food cake pan, Bundt pan, or four small loaf pans. Mix the wet ingredients and sugar in a bowl with electric mixer. In a separate bowl sift together dry ingredients. Add this to first mixture-do not over mix. Pour into pans. Fill pans 2/3 full. Bake for one hour at 350 degrees in one big pan or 45 minutes in loaf pans. Center should be firm. Cool on rack 30 minutes.

Submitted by-Chuck and Linda Duvall

Cooking Clips

ENGLISH MUFFIN CASSEROLE BREAD

1 package active dry yeast
1 tbsp. sugar
2 ½-3 cups sifted flour
1 tsp. salt
1 ¼ cups water
Cornmeal

In large mixer bowl, combine yeast and one cup of flour. In medium pan, heat water, sugar and salt till warm, stirring occasionally to dissolve the sugar. Add to dry mixture in mixing bowl. Beat with electric mixer, at low speed for ½ minute scraping sides of bowl. Beat 3 minutes at high speed. By hand, stir in just enough of the remaining flour to make a soft dough. Place dough in lightly greased bowl, turning over to grease surface. Cover, let rise in warm place till doubled in size, about 1 hour. Punch down & cover. Let rest 10 minutes. Grease 1 ½ qt. casserole dish. Sprinkle with cornmeal. Cover, let rise till doubled, about 45 min-1 hour. Uncover and bake in preheated 400 degree oven for 40-45 minutes. (If top browns to quickly, cover loosely with foil.) Remove from dish to cool.

Submitted by-John Neurohr

Cooking Clips

BEV BEADLES' CRESCENT AND CINNAMON ROLLS

1 cup sour cream
½ cup sugar
1 tsp. salt
1 stick (1/2 cup) margarine
2 pkgs. dry yeast
½ cup warm water
2 eggs
4 cups unsifted bread flour

Tools needed:
Mixmaster (or hand mixer-just a little harder with hand held mixer)
Small pan (for first four ingredients)
Small bowl (for eggs/beat slightly)
Bowl (for four cups flour)
Large bowl (for final dough to be refrigerated)
1 cup, ½ cup, 1 tsp. – measuring tools
Wooden spoon
Plastic scraper

Method: Warm sour cream, margarine, sugar, and salt in small pan. Pour water (1/2 cup warm) in mixing bowl. Sprinkle in yeast; stir to mix; wait for proofing action. Add heated mixture from small pan. Add beaten eggs. Mix gently. Add two cups flour; mix with mixmaster. Add last two cups flour by hand; stir with wooden spoon. When mostly mixed, put dough in clean bowl, cover with dishtowel and plate, and refrigerate for several hours (minimum of 3 hours).

TO MAKE CRESENT ROLLS:

Divide dough in half, roll out each half in circle shape on floured work surface. Cut pie shapes. Roll from large to small end to make crescents. Place on slightly greased baking sheet. Let rise 1- 1 ½ hours. Bake at 350° 12-15 minutes, brush with melted butter while hot. (They freeze wonderfully!)

Continued next page . . .

Cooking Clips

IF MAKING CINNAMON ROLLS:

Roll out each half, to shape of rectangle. Brush with margarine. Sprinkle liberally with mixture of brown sugar and cinnamon. Roll rectangle...long side to long side. Slice about every 1 ½ inches with a sharp knife. Place each roll in a greased muffin tin. Let rise 1-1 ½ hours; bake at 350° for 12-14 minutes. Top with frosting, made from 4x sugar/milk (2 cups 4x sugar+ appx. 2 tbsp. milk). Stir and frost.

"This bread is deliciously habit-forming. Beware and enjoy!"

Submitted by - Bev Beadles

Cooking Clips

CORN BREAD

Cream 1 stick butter
2 eggs well beaten
18 oz. carton sour cream
12 oz. Flako corn muffin mix
1 can whole kernel corn drained

Pour into 13 x 9 greased iron fry pan at 350 degrees for 50 minutes

Submitted by-Chuck and Linda Duvall

YELLOW SQUASH MUFFINS
Yield-1 ½ doz.

2 lbs. yellow squash (recipe say about 6-8 medium size)
2 eggs
1 cup margarine, melted
1 cup sugar
3 cups flour
1 tbsp. + 2 teaspoons baking powder
1 tsp. salt

Wash squash and cut into 1-inch slices. Cook in water until tender. Drain well and mash. Measure enough of squash to equal 2 cups.
Combine squash, eggs, and butter; stir well and set aside.
Combine remaining ingredients in large bowl; make a well in center of mix. Add squash mixture to dry ingredients, stirring just to moisten. Spoon into greased muffin pans, filling ¾ full. Bake at 375 degrees for 20 minutes, or until wooden pick inserted in center of muffin comes out clean.

Submitted by-Jerry Lindquist

SOUP

Cooking Clips

CURRIED LENTIL SOUP

With Granny Smith Apples and Sweet Italian Sausage

4 tbsp. butter
2 tbsp. Olive oil
1 large yellow onion, diced
2 cups chopped celery, including leaves
1 tbsp. curry powder
½ tsp. cumin
1/8 tsp. ground pepper
3 ½-4 qts. Chicken broth
1 16 oz. bag dried lentils
2 links sweet Italian sausage
1 tart Granny Smith apple
Hungarian paprika to garnish

In large saucepan, sauté onions and celery in butter and 1 tbsp. olive oil until just wilted, taking care not to burn. Add curry, cumin and pepper and continue to sauté. Add 3 ½ quarts chicken broth and bring to boil. Add lentils and bring back to boil. Reduce heat and simmer 15 minutes or until lentils begin to soften. Take care not to overcook.

Meanwhile, sauté sausages whole in remaining 1 tbsp. olive oil. Brown, but don't burn. When cooked though, remove from heat, drain and cool. Slice and quarter sausage pieces and add to broth.

Core, peel and dice and add to broth. Simmer all an additional 10 minutes. Add another ½ qt. chicken broth if needed to thin and simmer another 5 minutes. Adjust seasonings. Serve in soup plates or bowls with sprinkling of good quality Hungarian paprika to garnish. Serves 12.

James G. Harrison
Elizabeth Ruffin Harrison
And all the folks at Marks & Harrison

Cooking Clips

SANTA FE SOUP

2 lbs. ground beef
2 medium or large onions, chopped
3 (1 oz.) packets Taco seasoning mix
1 (1 oz.) packet Ranch dressing mix
1 (14-16 oz.) can dark red kidney beans (not drained)
1 (14-16 oz.) can black beans (not drained)
1 (14-16 oz.) can pinto beans (not drained)
2 (14-16 oz.) cans diced tomatoes with green chiles (not drained)
2 (14-16 oz.) cans white corn (not drained)
3 cups water

Cook meat and onions until meat is browned.

Drain grease.

Transfer to larger pot, if necessary.

Add all other ingredients.

Cover, bring to slow boil and simmer for 1 hour.

May be garnished with:

Sour cream, shredded cheddar cheese, sliced green onions

Serve with Tortilla chips.

Very easy, tastes great, even better when reheated, freezes well, and all ingredients may be increased or decreased to suit your individual taste.

Submitted by-Joe Chandler

Cooking Clips

KIP'S OYSTER STEW

2 tbsp. all-purpose flour	Dash hot sauce
2 tbsp. cold water	1 pint shucked oysters
1 ½ tsp. salt	¼ cup butter
1 tsp. Worcestershire sauce	2 cups 2% milk, scalded
1 can cream of celery soup (condensed)	

In saucepan blend flour, water, salt, Worcestershire, hot sauce and condensed soup. Stir in undrained oysters and butter. Simmer over very low heat, stirring gently until edges of oysters curl, 3 to 4 minutes. Add hot milk, remove from heat and cover. Let stand 15 minutes. Reheat briefly. Float pats of butter. Makes 4 servings

Submitted by-Andrew T. Moore, Jr.

LUCKY'S ROCKFISH CHOWDER

3 large potatoes
1 large onion
½ stick butter
1 lb. rockfish cubed
½ tsp. basil
2 cups water
1 cup half and half
½ tsp. salt
¼ tsp. pepper

Directions:
Sauté onions in butter.
Add all else except half and half.
Cook until potatoes are done.
Add half and half, cook 10-15 more minutes.

Submitted by-Stuart Lee

Cooking Clips

MEXICAN SOUP

Step 1: Pour two (32 oz. each) cartons of chicken broth into large pot.

Step 2: Add pre-cooked chicken (supermarket whole chicken, meat removed; or 3 boneless-skinless chicken breasts cut into strips; or 2-3 (6 oz.) packages of chicken strips.)

Step 3: Add 2 (15 oz.) cans of cannellini beans; a large jar of salsa Verde; and cumin to taste.

Step 4: Bring to boil and then simmer for one hour.

Step 5: Add grated cheese of choice and serve.

Submitted by - D. Kitchen

Cooking Clips

MEXICAN CHICKEN SOUP

A combination of various recipes by Mary Jo Kearfott, 2004
Serves 4 to 6 people

3 or 4 chicken breast halves, cubed
1 onion, chopped
2 cloves garlic, chopped
Fresh green chilies, roasted and peeled (or use 2 small cans)
1 tsp. chili powder
1 tsp. cumin
½ tsp. salt
1 quart chicken broth
½ cup salsa
Chopped cilantro to taste
1 can hominy or 1 can of black beans

Sauté onion and garlic in a little oil, remove from pan. Brown chicken. Add rest of ingredients, except cilantro and hominy/beans, and cook about one hour. Add hominy/beans and cilantro and cook for 15 minutes more. Freezes well. Garnish with shredded cheddar cheese, chopped green onions, sour cream, chopped cilantro, and sliced jalapeños.

Submitted by - Mary Jo Kearfott

Cooking Clips

TACO SOUP

2 lbs. ground beef, browned and drained
4 (15 oz.) cans diced tomatoes
2 cups water
8 oz. tomato sauce
2 (15 oz.) cans diced Rotel (tomatoes with green chilies)
2 (15 oz.) cans shoe peg corn
2 (15oz.) cans kidney beans
2 pkgs. taco seasoning
1 ½ pkgs. (dry) Hidden Valley Ranch dressing

Mix all in large pot. Simmer several hours.

Submitted by - JoAnn Pulliam, Office of U.S. Senator, Jim Webb

PASTAS, SAUCES & TOPPINGS

Cooking Clips

ERNESTA'S RED SAUCE

Approx. ½ cup olive oil
1 to 1 ¼ lbs ground beef
2 ½ Johnson Mild Italian sausages or Italian-flavored turkey sausages, skinned
Salt and pepper
6-7 medium garlic cloves
1 large stalk of celery
1 large carrot (or about 15 mini-peeled carrots)
Large handful of parsley leaves
1 semi-large onion
Small handful of basil leaves
5 pieces cloves
Salt and pepper
½ cup white wine
1 15-oz. can tomato sauce

(Will need a food processor for chopping and grinding)

In a large pot pour about 1 to 1 ¼ lbs. ground beef. Also add 2 ½ links of Johnson Mild Italian sausage links with skins removed and links broken into small chunks. Add salt and pepper. Cook meats until all pinkness disappears.

While meats are cooking:
Peel 6-7 garlic cloves
Clean and chop one large stalk of celery
Clean and chop one large carrot (or about 15 grocer's packaged "mini-peeled carrot sticks chopped)
Rinse one large handful of fresh parsley leaves (removing stems)
Chop one semi-large onion
Collect one small handful of fresh basil leaves

Grind all above vegetables in divided portions in food processor. Place ground mixture in large bowl.
Remove ground beef and sausage from pot retaining juice in pot.
Using food processor, ground beef in divided portions.
Place vegetable mixture in pot with retained juices. Add 5 pieces of cloves. Bring to a boil then lower heat to simmer at low boil for 25-30 minutes.
Add ground meats to vegetable mixture, add small amount of salt and pepper, ½ cup white wine, 2 15-oz. cans of tomato sauce and 3 cups water.

Continued, next page . . .

Cooking Clips

Bring to boil, then lower heat to simmering boil for 2-3 hours.

(Note: when serving with pasta, place 2 ladlefuls of sauce in bottom of serving dish, pour in cooked pasta, add more sauce as desired along with freshly grated parmesan cheese.)

Submitted by - Franco Ambrogi – "From the hills of Tuscany, my sister's sauce is truly Italian. Use it on pasta, in lasagna, or for a meat topping!"

Cooking Clips

GRILLED EGGPLANT MARINARA

2 large yellow onions, peeled and diced
½ tbsp. dried thyme
1 bunch fresh basil, chopped
1 bunch fresh parsley, finely chopped
½ cup red wine
4 meaty ripe tomatoes, chopped
2 pints cherry tomatoes, whole
1 medium red bell pepper, chopped
salt and pepper to taste
1 large eggplant
1/3 cup olive oil
5-6 cloves of garlic, minced (about 2 tbsp.)
1 tbsp. dried oregano
Mozzarella cheese plank
Wild mushroom tortellini (recommended)
Grated Parmesan cheese

Sauce:
In large soup pot, heat up the olive oil. Add the onions and cook slowly, on medium heat until they start to caramelize. They should be evenly brown and soft. Cooking them this way brings out the natural sweetness in onions. Add the garlic, fresh and dried herbs and cook for 5 minutes. Deglaze the pan with the ½ cup of red wine and cook for 2 minutes more. Add the tomatoes and red pepper and stir to combine. Bring to a simmer and cook on slow, stirring occasionally for about 3 hours until desired thickness is achieved. Add salt and pepper to taste.

Eggplant:
Place eggplant on its side and cut into half inch thick slabs. Brush both sides of each slab with olive oil and sprinkle with salt and pepper. Over medium charcoal heat (no flame), grill on one side until underside is brown. Turn and place quarter-inch slice of mozzarella on grilled side. Place lid on grill until reverse side is grilled and cheese is melted.

This dish may be served over your favorite pasta, and it's particularly tasty over wild mushroom tortellini and topped with freshly ground Parmesan.

Submitted by - Bo Bowden

ITALIAN BEEF RAGU

2 tablespoons olive oil
1 cup chopped onion
2 cans (about 14 ounces each) fire-roasted diced tomatoes
1 teaspoon dried oregano
1 teaspoon dried basil
1/8 teaspoon red pepper flakes or black pepper
1 package (about 17 ounces) fully cooked beef pot roast (see notes)
8 oz. uncooked fettuccine

1. Heat oil in large saucepan over medium heat. Add onion; cook and stir 5 minutes or until translucent and slightly browned, stirring occasionally.
Add tomatoes, oregano, basil and red pepper flakes; bring to a boil over high heat. Reduce heat; simmer, uncovered, 10 minutes, stirring occasionally.
2. Remove pot roast from package; add au jus to tomato mixture; simmer 5 to 10 minutes or until heated through.
3. Meanwhile, cook fettuccine according to package directions; drain,. Divide fettuccine among 4 serving plates; top with beef Ragu.

Makes 4 servings

Submitted by - Tom Bliley, Former Congressman

Cooking Clips

CUCUMBER-CORIANDER YOGURT SAUCE

2¼ cups plain whole-milk yogurt
1 cup unpeeled English hothouse cucumber, finely chopped
½ cup fresh cilantro, chopped
1 tbsp. coriander seeds, coarsely cracked
1 tbsp. fresh lemon juice

Stir all ingredients in medium bowl to blend. Season to taste with salt and pepper. Do ahead. Can be made one day in advance. Cover and refrigerate.

Submitted by - Ray and Connie Sorrell

CRANBERRY BUTTER

1 (12 oz.) bag fresh cranberries
2 cups sugar (or a little more, depending on taste)
3 sticks (1½ cups) butter, softened
Grated peel of one orange

Place cranberries in a medium saucepan - low heat. Add ½ cup water and sprinkle in the sugar. Simmer, stirring occasionally, for 30 minutes or so – or until berries are mushy and water evaporates. Transfer to a bowl to cool. Place butter in mixing bowl and beat on low speed until fluffy. Add cranberries and beat until well combined. Serve at room temperature on bagels, toast, or biscuits. Makes a great gift with a loaf of homemade bread.

Submitted by - JoAnn Pulliam, Office of U.S. Senator, Jim Webb

Cooking Clips

LIP-SMACKIN' FETA VINAIGRETTE

1 tbsp. lemon juice
3 tbsp. red wine vinegar
¾ cup oil
1 tbsp. dried oregano
1½ tsp. Cavender's Greek Seasoning
2 cloves garlic
½ cup feta (cheese)

Combine all ingredients in blender or food processor or mash feta with fork and mix. Great on a salad of greens (your choice): tomatoes, Vidalia onions (lots), cucumbers (lots) and black olives (optional). Extra feta can be added to top of salad.

Submitted by - JoAnn Pulliam, Office of U.S. Senator, Jim Webb

Cooking Clips

HONEY-MUSTARD DILL SAUCE

1 cup mayonnaise
¾ cup hot honey mustard
2/3 cup fresh dill, chopped

Stir all ingredients in medium bowl to blend. Season to taste with salt and pepper. Do ahead. Can be made one day in advance. Cover and refrigerate.

Submitted by - Ray and Connie Sorrell

DESSERTS

BLACKBERRY ROLL

Use about 1 qt. of blackberries

Cut together:
2 cups flour
2-½ tsp. baking powder
1 ¼ tsp. salt
1 tbsp. sugar
3 tsp. butter

Add ¾ cup of milk. You sometimes have to add a little more flour so it won't be too sticky to roll out.

Roll out on wax paper, then brush with soft or melted butter.
Lay ½ of the blackberries on crust and sprinkle with ½ tsp. cinnamon mixed with ½ cup sugar.

Roll up like a jelly roll and put in a greased Pyrex casserole dish or pan. (This is the hardest part, but the wax paper will help.)

Put rest of blackberries around the roll. Add about ¼ cup of water and sprinkle ½ cup sugar over roll and blackberries. Bake at 425 degrees for 30 minutes.

Delicious served with ice cream or boiled custard.

Submitted by-Jerry Lindquist

Cooking Clips

MY MOTHER'S POUND CAKE

½ pound country butter (this was when butter came in round cakes-now you just use 2 sticks.)
1 stick margarine
3 cups sugar
3 ½ cups of flour (I found several copies of this recipe and some said 3 1/3 cups. Maybe it doesn't matter!)
1 tsp. baking powder
1 cup milk
1 ½ tsp. lemon flavoring
½ tsp. almond flavoring
5 eggs
1/8 tsp. salt

Cream butter, margarine and sugar. Beat in eggs one at a time. Add dry ingredients, then milk and flavorings. Beat well.

Pour into large greased and floured tube or Bundt pan.

Bake in preheated 300 degrees oven for 1½ hours. Cool on rack.

Submitted by-Jerry Lindquist

Cooking Clips

ICE CREAM CAKE

1 half gallon vanilla ice cream (I use Breyer's Vanilla Bean, Light)
1 ½ cups graham cracker crumbs
4 tbsp. sherry (optional)
Frozen whipped topping (thawed)
Grated coconut
Fresh strawberries

Soften ice cream. Stir in graham cracker crumbs and sherry. Freeze in a loaf pan. When hard frozen, unmold and ice with whipped topping. Sprinkle with shredded coconut and garnish with mint leaves and fresh strawberries. Slice to serve. Serves 6-8

This is one of my favorite company desserts. You can double the recipe and freeze in a tube pan. (I don't double the quantity of sherry.) Serve at the table. It is so pretty and guests think you have worked so hard!
At Christmas I have garnished it with maraschino cherries and holly leaves instead of strawberries.

Submitted by-Jerry Lindquist
Commentary by wife Mary Trew (that's her 1st. name.)

HUXOLL APPLE CAKE

2 cups sugar
1 ¼ cups vegetable oil
3 eggs
2 tsp. vanilla
3 cups flour
1 tsp. baking soda
1 tsp. cinnamon
¼ tsp. salt
3 cups diced apples
1 cup chopped nuts

Mix sugar and oil. Add eggs and vanilla and mix well. Add flour one cup at a time and mix.
Add baking soda, cinnamon and salt, and mix.
Gently mix in apples and nuts. Pour into well-greased 10" tube pan. Bake in preheated oven at 350 degrees for 1 or 1 ¼ hours depending on oven. Allow to cool 20 minutes before removing from pan. Glaze if desired.

GLAZE: Melt together 1/8 cup butter, ¼ cup brown sugar, and 1/8 cup milk. Pour glaze over warm cake.

Submitted by-Ron Rash
From Anita

Cooking Clips

BLUEBERRY BOY BAIT

2 cups all purpose flour
1 ½ cups sugar
2 teaspoons baking powder
1 teaspoon salt
2/3 cup butter, softened
1 cup milk
2 eggs
1 cup blueberries, frozen, fresh or drained canned
¼ cup sugar
½ teaspoon cinnamon

13 x 9 inch cake
Oven 350 degrees

In large mixer bowl, combine flour, sugar, baking powder, salt, butter, milk and eggs. Blend at low speed until dry ingredients are moistened; beat at medium speed for 3 minutes. Pour into greased and floured 13 x 9-inch pan. Arrange blueberries on top. Combine sugar and cinnamon; sprinkle over the top. Bake at 350 degrees for 40 to 50 minutes or until cake springs back when touched lightly in center. Cut in squares and serve warm or cold with whipped cream or ice cream. Delicious one-step coffee cake or serve for dessert. (Pillsbury's 1976)

Submitted by-Charlene K. Boynton

GREAT CHOCOLATE CAKE

1 cup sugar
4 eggs
1 cup all-purpose flour
1 tsp. baking powder
1 tsp vanilla
1 pound can chocolate syrup

Mix all ingredients together and pour into greased 10" x 14" pan.
Bake at 350 degrees for 25 minutes.
Before the cake is done, start making the frosting.

Frosting:

On stove top, heat in pan to boiling point –

1 stick butter (1/2 cup)
1/3 cup evaporated milk
1 cup sugar

Mix all ingredients and cook for about 2 minutes until boiling.
Remove from heat.
Stir in 6 ounces chocolate chips and ½ cup chopped nuts (optional).
Pour over cake immediately after removing cake from oven.
Cool all.

Submitted by - Carolyn and Randy Ridgely

Cooking Clips

PECAN SHORTBREAD

¾ pound unsalted butter, at room temperature
1 cup sugar
1 tsp. pure vanilla extract
1 tsp. pure almond extract
3 ½ cups all-purpose flour
¼ tsp. salt
1 ½ cups small, diced pecans

Preheat oven to 350 degrees.

In the bowl of an electric mixer fitted with a paddle attachment, mix together butter and sugar until just combined.
Add vanilla and almond extracts.
In medium bowl, sift together the flour and salt, then add them to the butter/sugar mixture.
Add pecans and mix on low speed until dough starts to come together.
Dump onto a surface dusted with flour and shape into flat disk.
Wrap in plastic and chill for 30 minutes.

Roll dough ½ -inch thick, and cut into 2 ½-inch squares with plain or fluted cutter (or cut into any shape you like with cookie cutter, etc.)
Place cookies on ungreased baking sheet.

Bake 20 – 25 minutes, until edges begin to brown. Allow to cool to room temperature and serve.

Cooking Clips

RANGER COOKIES

1 cup shortening
1 cup sugar
1 cup packed brown sugar
2 eggs
1 tsp. vanilla extract
2 cups all-purpose flour
1 tsp. baking soda
½ tsp. baking powder
½ tsp. salt
2 cups quick-cooking oats
2 cups crisp rice cereal
1 cup flaked coconut

In large mixing bowl, cream shortening and sugars until light and fluffy.
Beat in eggs and vanilla.
Combine flour, baking soda, baking powder, and salt.
Gradually add to creamed mixture and mix well.
Stir in oats, cereal, and coconut.
Drop by rounded tablespoonfuls - 2 inches apart - onto ungreased baking sheets.
Bake at 350 degrees for 7-9 minutes or until golden brown.
Remove to wire racks.
Makes about 7 ½ dozen cookies

Submitted by - Carolyn and Randy Ridgely – "Great!"

Cooking Clips

SOUR CREAM POUND CAKE

1 cup Crisco (or Shortening)
1 cup sour cream
3 cups sugar
¼ tsp. soda
6 eggs
3 cups sifted cake flour
1 tsp. vanilla
1 tsp. lemon or almond extract
¼ tsp. salt

Cream Crisco/shortening, sour cream, and sugar.
Add eggs, flour (soda and salt).
Beat 4 minutes on medium
Add extract.
Grease and flour tube cake pan or Bundt cake pan.
Bake 1 hour on 325 degrees

Icing

½ box "10 x powered sugar"
1 tsp. lemon or almond extract
1 tsp. vanilla extract
2 tbsp. milk
½ stick (4 Tbsp.) butter

Mix all ingredients together and heat over low temperature; pour over cake while still hot.

Submitted by - Carolyn and Randy Ridgely – "Bob Barton's mother's pound cake – delicious!"

Cooking Clips

APPLE AND CHEDDAR CHEESE FLAN
Preheat oven to 400 degrees
2 in. flan or pie pan

Almond Pie Crust:
Top – make 2 days ahead, cover, refrigerate until ready to make
½ cup whole almonds (unblanched)
20 arrowroot or vanilla cookies
1/3 cup butter
2 tbsp. cane sugar
Filling:
6 apples
1 cup sour cream
¼ cup creamed cottage cheese
1 large egg, beaten
2 cups finely shredded cheddar cheese
½ cup cane sugar
1 tbsp. chopped fresh sweet cicely or meat

1 Almond Pie Crust: In food processor or blender, combine almonds and cookies. Process for 20 seconds or until medium-fine

2. In saucepan, melt butter over medium heat. Remove from heat, stir in almond mixture and sugar. Press crumb crust into pan. Chill until ready to fill.

3. Filling: Peel, core and slice 5 apples. In large bowl, mix sour cream and cottage cheese together. Beat in egg. Add sliced apple, cheddar cheese, sugar and sweet cicely (or mint) and stir well.

4. Spoon cheese mixture over almond pie crust, spreading to level the top core and thinly slice remaining apple, leaving the peel on. Arrange over top of filling. Bake in preheated oven for 1 hour or until crust is lightly brown and apples are tender, let sit for 10 minutes before serving.

Submitted by-Buddy Crowder
Tommy Streat

Cooking Clips

HAY STACK COOKIES

1 12 oz. bag chocolate bits
1 12 oz. bag butterscotch bits
1 cup Spanish peanuts
1 3 oz. can chow mien noodles

Melt and mix in nuts and noodles. Mix until covered. Drop by teaspoonful onto waxed paper. Let set until firm.

Submitted by-Fil Forrest

Cooking Clips

CHRIS MILLER'S CHOCOLATE PIE

3 tsp. butter
1 cup sugar
¼ cup flour
1 egg beaten
1 ¼ cup milk
2 squares chocolate
1 tsp. vanilla
1 8" baked pie shell

Cream butter and sugar, add flour, combine with beaten eggs and milk and chocolate in top of a double boiler. Cook until thick and smooth. Remove, pour into pie shell. Cool in refrigerator. Top with whipped cream.

Submitted by-Chris Miller

Cooking Clips

COCONUT PIE

1 1/3 cup sugar
1 tsp. vanilla flavoring
1 sm. can Carnation evaporated milk
1 cup Angel Flake coconut
¼ stick margarine, melted
2 eggs, beaten

Combine above ingredients. Pour into unbaked pie shell. Bake at 350 degrees for 1 hour.

Submitted by-Jackie and Jay Snoddy

Cooking Clips

GRANDMOTHERS PORK CAKE

1 LB. freshly ground pork fat, no lean, no salt
1 qt. boiling hot water
4 cups brown sugar
8 cups all purpose flour
1 lb. dark raisins
1 lb. white raisins
1 lb. currants-optional
1 cup nuts, English walnut
1 tbsp. cloves
1 tbsp. all spice
1 tbsp. nutmeg
1 tsp. ginger
1 tbsp. baking soda
¼ cup cold water
Mix accordingly

Pour boiling hot water over pork fat and brown sugar. Let cool. Sift flour and spices together, add raisins, nuts to flour and stir into water, sugar, meat mixture, beat well. Last, dissolve soda in cold water, stir into the cake batter, mix well. Bake in angel cake pans lined with oiled brown paper or waxed paper will do. 1 large or 2 medium size pans-Bake in slow oven 275-300 degrees for two hours-Cool well before storing

½ cup peach brandy poured over top of cakes keep them moist.
(Anonymous)

Cooking Clips

MAC & CHARLIE SUSKIND'S MAGNIFICENT HOT FUDGE SAUCE

Ingredients:
2 (1 oz) squares of softened unsweetened chocolate
½ cup sugar
1 ¼ cup sugar
Pinch salt
5 or 6 oz. can evaporated milk
1 tbsp. vanilla
3 tbsp. Karo syrup

Mix all ingredients together (except the vanilla)
Bring to a boil for 5 minutes
Take off stove and add vanilla
Cool slightly
Pour over ice cream and have a rockin good time
Store in refrigerator

Submitted by-Mac & Charlie Suskind

Cooking Clips

GREG SUSKIND'S CHEWY CHOCOLATE CHIP COOKIES

Ingredients

2 cups softened butter

2 cups brown sugar

6 tbsp. sugar

3 large eggs

4 tsp. vanilla

¾ cup milk

4 cups flour

1 tsp. baking soda

1 tsp. baking powder

12 oz. bag chocolate chips

12 oz. bag white chocolate chips

*** Add cup of Heath Bar chips if you want

What To Do:

Preheat oven to 300 degrees

Cream butter and sugars

Beat in eggs, vanilla extract, and milk

In mixing bowl, mix dry ingredients and beat into butter mixture at low speed.

Stir in the chocolate and white chocolate chips

Drop cookie dough onto cookie sheet covered with parchment

Paper (space cookies 3 inches apart)

Bake for 15 minutes
***Makes 4 dozen cookies
Submitted by-Greg Suskind

Cooking Clips

BEST GOOEY BROWNIES

1 (12-oz.) package semisweet chocolate chips
1 can sweetened condensed milk (not evaporated milk)
½ lb. (2 sticks) plus 2 tablespoons sugar
1 lb (2 ¼ cups packed) brown sugar
2 eggs
1 tsp. vanilla extract
2 cups all-purpose flour
1 tsp. salt
¾ cup pecans or walnuts, chopped

Preheat the oven to 350 degrees. Lightly oil a 13 x 9 x 2 inch baking pan.

In large sauce pan over low heat, melt chocolate chips with condensed milk and 2 tablespoons of butter while stirring slowly. Remove from heat and cool slightly. Melt remaining half pound of butter, stir in sugar, and add to chocolate mixture. Beat in eggs one at a time. Stir in vanilla, flour, and salt; fold in the nuts.

Turn mixture into prepared pan and bake for 30 to 35 minutes. Do not overbake—this is best if still gooey in the center. Cut while warm. These are divine if cut into larger squares and served with ice cream as a dessert. Makes 24 large brownies.

Submitted by-Joyce & Walford Crenshaw

STRAWBERRY TOPPED CHEESE CAKE

Crust:
1 ½ cup graham cracker crumbs
¼ cup sugar
1/3 melted butter
Combine crumbs, sugar and butter-press to 9" pie pan

Cheese Cake:
1 lb. Philadelphia cream cheese (2 large packages)
¾ cup sugar
3 eggs
1 tsp. vanilla
Blend cheese, sugar and vanilla
Beat in eggs with beater until smooth and creamy
Pour into crust and bake in 350 degree oven for 35 minutes (or until firm)
Glaze:
1 ten oz. package frozen strawberries (thawed)
½ tsp. corn starch
1 teaspoon fresh lemon juice
Red coloring (drop or two to redden strawberries)
Place corn starch in sauce pan and gradually add berries (get the sliced variety)
Bring to boil and cook until thick and clear
Add coloring – remove from flame
Add lemon juice
Set aside to cool
Spread on top of cooled cake

(Keep in refrigerator)

Submitted by-Carl and Priscilla Ohallahan

Cooking Clips

CHOCOLATE CAKE

Mix:
2 cups flour   2 cups sugar

Boil for 1 minute, stirring constantly:
1 cup water   1 stick (1/2 cup) margarine
1 cup cooking oil   4 tbsp. cocoa

Mix flour and sugar into above mixture and then add:
½ cup buttermilk   1 tsp. soda
2 eggs   pinch of salt

Bake at 350° for 30 to 40 minutes in 10" x 15" pan.

Icing:
4 tbsp. cocoa   4 tbsp. milk
1 stick (1/2 cup) margarine   1 tsp. Vanilla extract

Bring icing to a boil and add one box of powdered sugar, then pour over cake while hot

Submitted by - Tom & Jeanne Hughes, Mechanicsville, VA

APPLE CAKE

½ cup butter (1 stick.)
2 cups sugar
2 eggs
1 tsp. vanilla extract
2 cups cake flour
1 tsp. nutmeg
1 tsp. cinnamon
1 tsp. salt
1 tsp. baking soda
1 cup raisins
1 cup pecans or walnuts, chopped
4 cups apples. Diced
Cool Whip or lemon sauce topping

Cream butter and sugar; add beaten eggs and vanilla. Add flour, spices, salt, and soda to the creamed mixture, then add raisins, nuts, and apples. Bake at 300° for 45 minutes in a lightly greased pan (13" x 9"). Winesap or McIntosh apples are preferred. Serve with Cool Whip or lemon sauce, or combine about a half stick of margarine with some brown sugar and place on top of baked cake. Broil for a very short time to make a crisp sweet topping (watch carefully as it browns).

Submitted by - Tom and Jeanne Hughes

Cooking Clips

SWEET POTATO CUSTARD PIE

2 eggs
¼ cup sugar
½ tsp. vanilla extract
1½ cups milk
¼ tsp. cinnamon or nutmeg
½ tsp. salt
1½ cups sweet potatoes, cooked

Mix sugar, salt, and vanilla extract. Gradually add sweet potatoes, eggs (slightly beaten), cinnamon or nutmeg, and milk. Bake at 425° for 40 minutes. Garnish with cinnamon or nutmeg.

Submitted by - C. Wayne Anderson

OLD FASHIONED BOILED CUSTARD

1 cup sugar
2 tbsp. flour
2 eggs
2 cups milk
1 tsp. vanilla

Mix sugar and flour in 2 qt. saucepan and stir well to remove all lumps.
Add eggs, one at a time, stirring well.
Add milk slowly, stirring.
Cook over medium heat until custard coats spoon.
Remove from heat and add vanilla.
Refrigerate.
Makes 1-½ pints.

This is wonderful over blackberry roll, but is also good over pound cake. Or, you can just eat it by itself. My mother said her mother used to make this as a desert and they ate it warm.

Submitted by-Jerry Lindquist

ALAN'S GINGERSNAPS

1½ cups butter-flavored Crisco
2 cups sugar
2 eggs
½ cup molasses
4 cups flour
2 tsp. baking soda
2 heaping tsp. EACH ground cinnamon, cloves, and ginger
¾ cup sugar (for rolling)

In a large mixing bowl, beat together shortening and sugar, until light and fluffy. Thoroughly mix in eggs and molasses. Sift together flour, baking soda, cinnamon, cloves, and ginger. Blend gradually into batter. Roll dough into small balls. Roll balls in sugar to coat. Place on greased cookie sheets and bake in preheated 350-degree oven until top of cookies crack, about 7-8 minutes.

Submitted by - Alan Gayle

CHOCOLATE CHIP CHEESECAKE

1 cup graham cracker crumbs
3 tbsp. sugar
3 tbsp. butter, melted
3 (8 oz.) packages cream cheese, softened
¾ cup sugar
3 eggs
1 cup mini semi-sweet chocolate chips
1 tsp. vanilla extract

Combine graham crumbs, sugar and butter. Press into 9" spring form pan. Beat cream cheese and sugar with electric mixer on medium speed. Add eggs and mix until just blended. Blend in vanilla extract. Stir in chocolate chips. Pour over crust. Bake at 450° for 10 minutes. Reduce heat to 250° and bake for 35 minutes. Chill.

Submitted by - Billie Dew – sister of Larry Jones

Cooking Clips

PECAN PIE

3 eggs, lightly beaten
1 tsp. vanilla extract
1 cup Karo syrup (½ cup light and ½ cup dark)
4 tbsp. butter, melted
½ tsp. salt
1 cup pecan halves
1 pie crust

Beat together the ingredients, except the pecans. Stir in the pecans, and pour mixture into an unbaked pie crust. Bake at 350° for 40 minutes.

"Every year at Christmas, I make this special pie, and my husband, Don Mann, takes it to Hugh Campbell at the John Marshall Barber shop. Every time Hugh says. 'it's the best one!' The recipe is from my mother, who grew up in North Carolina in a home surrounded by pecan trees. She would pick up nuts from the yard and make a pie. Those fresh golden pecans made a beautiful and delicious pie."

Submitted by - Don and Dianne Mann

CHOCOLATE GUINNESS CAKE

CAKE
1 cup Guinness stout (not the whole can)
1 stick (1/2 cup) unsalted butter (I substituted Earth Balance brand shortening seamlessly), sliced
¾ cup unsweetened cocoa powder
2 cups granulated sugar (superfine, if possible)
¾ cup sour cream (I substituted plain yogurt without a hitch)
2 eggs
1 tbsp. vanilla extract
2 cups all-purpose flour
2½ tsp. baking soda

ICING
8 oz. cream cheese
1 cup confectioner's sugar
½ cup heavy cream

Preheat oven to 350°. Butter a 9"springform pan and line bottom with parchment paper. Pour Guinness into a large saucepan, add butter and heat until melted. Whisk in cocoa powder and sugar. In a small bowl, beat sour cream with eggs and vanilla and then pour into brown, buttery, beery mixture, and finally, whisk in flour and baking soda. Pour cake batter into greased and lined pan and bake for 45 minutes to an hour (check at 45 minutes for doneness, poking a skewer in center). Leave to cool completely in the pan on a cooling rack, as it is quite a damp cake. When cake is cold, gently peel off parchment paper and transfer to a platter or cake stand. Place cream cheese and confectioner's sugar in a mixing bowl, and whip with an electric beater until smooth (you may also do this with a food processor). Add cream and beat again, until you have a spreadable consistency. Ice top of cake, starting at middle and fanning out, so that it resembles the frothy top of the famous pint.

Yields about 12 slices.
Submitted by - John S. Davis via "Feast" by Nigella Lawson

Cooking Clips

CREAM PIE

1 cup milk
2 cups cream
2 eggs
1 tbsp. cornstarch
1 tsp. vanilla extract
1/2 cup sugar

Mix sugar and cornstarch. Add beaten eggs, leaving white of one. Heat cream and milk to a boil; add to first mixture and keep stirring. Return to stove to thicken; add vanilla. Pour into thick, rich crust. Beat white of egg to a stiff froth; add a pinch of sugar. Brown in oven.

Submitted by - John C. Davis

Cooking Clips

CREAM CHEESE FROSTING

16 oz. package powdered sugar
8 oz. block cream cheese, softened
½ cup (1 stick) butter, softened, not melted
2 tsp. vanilla extract

Cream all four ingredients together until well blended. Spread on cake.

Submitted by - Robert Zehmer, Glen Allen, VA (given to him by his mother, Elizabeth Zehmer, and handed down from his grandmother, Ann Cameron Williams.)

Cooking Clips

OLD FASHION POUND CAKE

2 ½ sticks (1 ½ cups) butter
4 oz. golden (yellow) Crisco (shortening)
3 cups sugar
5 eggs
3 1/3 cups cake flour (Swansdown)
1 tsp. baking powder
½ tsp. salt
1 cup whipping cream
3 tsp. vanilla extract

Cream sugar, butter, and shortening well. Add eggs, one at a time, beating well each time to mix. Add flour, salt, and baking powder together. Add whipping cream and vanilla to mixture as well. Bake in a large tube (cake) pan, which has been greased with butter and flour. Bake at 300°for two hours. (Recommended with Cream Cheese Frosting recipe, which follows.)

Submitted by - Robert Zehmer, Glen Allen, VA (given to him by his mother, Elizabeth Zehmer, and handed down from his grandmother, Ann Cameron Williams.)

Cooking Clips

RUSINGA'S BANOFFEE PIE

Digestive biscuits or graham crackers, crushed
Butter, melted
Condensed milk
Whipping cream, whipped
Bananas, sliced
Drinking chocolate powder

Boil the condensed milk (in the tin with a hole at the top) for 1 ½ hours, then leave to cool. (Or, heat more quickly by pouring into a bowl and microwaving for three - four minutes.) Meanwhile, pour the melted butter over the crushed biscuits/graham crackers and combine. Line the bottom of a flan dish with the biscuit/graham cracker mix. When cooled, pour the condensed milk over the biscuit/graham cracker base. Top with sliced bananas. Add the whipping cream on top of the bananas and then sprinkle with drinking chocolate powder.

Submitted by - Ronald W. Davis

PUMPKIN PIE CAKE

1 (16 oz.) can pumpkin
1 (12 oz.) can evaporated milk
1½ cups white sugar
4 eggs
1 tsp. cinnamon

Mix together all ingredients above.

1 yellow cake mix
2 sticks (1 cup) butter, melted
1/2 cup pecans, chopped

Pour pumpkin mixture into 9" x 13" pan. Sprinkle dry cake mix on top. Drizzle chopped pecans over all. Bake at 350° for 60-75 minutes.

Submitted by - Ronald W. Davis

CHOCOLATE MOUSSE CAKE

12 oz. chocolate wafers, crushed
4 eggs, separated
½ cup butter, melted
1 tsp. vanilla extract
16 oz. semi-sweet chips
4 cups whipping cream
2 eggs
10 tbsp. powdered sugar
Chocolate curls to garnish

Combine wafers and butter. Press on bottom and sides of greased spring form pan. Chill. Melt chocolate chips in double boiler (or microwave). Add whole eggs. Mix well. Add yolks. Mix well. Add vanilla. Beat 2 cups cream until soft peaks form. Add 6 tbsp. powdered sugar and beat until stiff. Beat egg whites until stiff. Fold whipped cream and whites into chocolate mixture until well blended. Pour into crust. Chill overnight. May be frozen at this point. (The texture of this mousse is actually better when it is slightly frozen.) Whip remaining 2 cups cream and 4 tbsp. sugar until stiff. Loosen crust from sides of pan with knife. Top with sweetened whipped cream. Garnish with chocolate curls or chocolate leaves.

"I'm fairly sure they serve this in Heaven."

Submitted by - JoAnn Pulliam, Office of U.S. Senator, Jim Webb

MA'S GOOD OLE MOLASSES COOKIES

2 sticks oleo (or margarine)
2 cups sugar
2 eggs
½ cup molasses (Gold Label brand)
3 cups flour
4 tsp. baking soda
½ tsp. salt
2 tsp. cinnamon
1 ½ tsp. ginger
1 ½ tsp. cloves

Melt shortening, add sugar and cool. Add molasses and eggs. Sift flour with ginger and mix into mixture. Roll by teaspoonful in flour. Bake 8 to 10 minutes at 375°. Sift on powdered sugar while warm.

Submitted by - Linwood Holton, "Here's the best recipe you will receive. It's Dwight Holton's favorite and comes with an assist by Jinks. P.S. Ignore the print on back of [the original] recipe; that's how we conservatives save paper!"

Submitted by – Linwood Holton, Loyal Customer

BROWNIE TORTE

1 cup mini-choc. chips (l pkg. semi-sweet mini-choc chips)
2/3 cup butter
1 cup sugar
1 cup all-purpose flour
1 tsp. baking powder
1 tsp. salt
4 eggs
1 tsp. vanilla
1 cup chopped nuts (pecans or walnuts)

Line jelly roll pan with greased wax paper or plain parchment paper. Melt 1 cup mini-choc. chips and 2/3 cup butter in 3 quart saucepan or double boiler over medium heat. Remove from heat and add sugar, mix well, add eggs, mix well, add flour, baking powder & salt, mix well, add vanilla and nuts, mix well. Pour mixture onto lined jelly roll pan and bake 20-25 minutes at 350°. Cool for 10 minutes before removing from pan. Cool completely before icing. Cut in four equal parts.

Icing

2 cups heavy whipping cream
1/4 cup powdered sugar
1 tsp. vanilla
2/3 cup mini-choc chips

Beat first three ingredients until stiff. Stir in mini-choc chips and ice brownie torte. Refrigerate for 1 hour before serving.

Cooking Clips

RICH CHOCOLATE CAKE

9 oz. semisweet chocolate, chopped
1 cup unsalted butter, cut into pieces
5 eggs
½ cup superfine sugar, plus 1 tbsp. and some for sprinkling
1 tbsp. cocoa powder
2 tsp.. vanilla extract
Cocoa powder, for dusting, and
Chocolate shavings, to decorate

Preheat oven to 325 degrees. Lightly butter 9" springform cake pan and line case with nonstick baking paper. Butter paper and sprinkle with little sugar, then tap out excess sugar.

The cake is baked in bain-marie. Carefully surround bottom and sides of pan with double thickness of foil to prevent water from leaking into cake.

Melt chocolate and butter in saucepan over low heat until smooth, stirring frequently, and remove from heat. Beat eggs and ½ cup sugar with electric mixer for 1 minute. Mix together cocoa and l tbsp. sugar and add to egg mixture blending well. Beat in vanilla extract and slowly blend in chocolate mixture. Pour into prepared pan and tap lightly to remove air bubbles.

Place cake pan in roasting pan and add boiling water to come up ¾ " of the pan. Bake for 45- 50 min. or until a skewer inserted 2" from edge comes out clean. Remove cake from roasting pan and remove foil and sides of pan to cool completely. Invert on wire rack and remove base of pan and paper. Dust cake liberally with cocoa and decorate edge with chocolate shavings.

Cooking Clips

SUSAN ALLEN'S FAMOUS CRANBERRY COOKIES

(Passed down from her Lithuanian Grandmother)

½ cup butter
1 cup sugar
¾ cup firmly packed brown sugar
¼ cup milk
2 tbsp. orange juice
1 egg
3 cups all-purpose flour
1 tsp. baking powder
¼ tsp. baking soda
½ tsp. salt
1 cup chopped nuts
2 ½ cups chopped fresh cranberries (easiest to chop if frozen)

*Preheat oven to 375 degrees
Beat butter and sugar in large bowl until creamy.
Combine milk, orange juice and egg in separate large bowl and mix well.
Add flour, baking powder, baking soda and salt and mix well.
Stir flour mixture into creamed mixture and blend well.
Fold in nuts and cranberries.
Drop by spoonful onto greased cookie sheet.
Bake 10-15 minutes
Makes 12 dozen

Submitted by – Susan Allen